Hero Horse

Jenny Hughes

Hero Horse

Cover and inside illustrations: © 2008 Jennifer Bell
Cover layout: Stabenfeldt A/S

Typeset by Roberta L. Melzl
Editor: Bobbie Chase
Printed in Germany, 2008

ISBN: 978-1-933343-84-6

Available exclusively through PONY Book Club.

Chapter ONE

Cheers and shouts of congratulation were still ringing in my ears as Scarlet and I left the crowd behind us. I led her quietly across the deserted stretch of grass toward our trailer, feeling the warmth from her gleaming chestnut shoulder as she pressed against me.

"There," I said, swiftly taking off her saddle and rubbing the tired muscles beneath it. "Is that better?"

She nudged me affectionately with her soft velvet nose and for a minute or two we stood locked together, my arms wrapped tight around her neck.

"You were wonderful," I told her. "You're the best pony anyone ever had and I'm the luckiest girl in the world."

"Do you know, Dana, I always wondered what you said to your horse after winning a class." My friend Lucy had arrived just behind me. "I always figured you were going through the technicalities of each jump – never guessed it was all sappy stuff!"

"I'm just telling Scarlet the truth," I said as I lifted my head and turned to grin at her. "Did you *see* the way she cut seconds off our time with that last turn?"

"Yeah, the whole place went wild, didn't it?" Lucy shook back her sleek curtain of hair. "The team from Barton Pony Club was sure they'd beaten us but because of you, *our* club's won the Challenge Cup for the first time ever."

"Because of Scarlet, you mean," I said, giving my gorgeous pony another kiss. "She's been great all day."

"You haven't been bad yourself," Lucy smiled saucily. "I wouldn't have even gone *into* a ring with jumps that high, let alone flown around them against the clock. Everyone's saying you've got nerves of steel."

"I don't know about that," I said, massaging my horse's back gently. "I guess I take it all a little seriously, but I really love competing and I know Scarlet does too."

"Yeah I can see she does," said Lucy as she patted my chestnut's neck and picked up a grooming kit. "I suppose you'll be spending the whole summer vacation either practicing or competing in local shows?"

"That's the plan," I agreed. "I mean, helping the team win the Inter-Club Competition is the total highlight but I still want to do more."

Lucy, as usual, had started helping get my pony ready for the trip home. "Yeah, like you said, you take competing seriously, don't you?"

"Well sure," I said, surprised. "There's nothing wrong with that, is there? Or do you think I'm boring and should lighten up?"

I was only joking but I could see from the expression on my friend's face that something like that had definitely crossed her mind.

"Um," she looked a bit embarrassed. "You're not *dull*, I mean you're always up to something. You're just getting kind of single minded and focused. A little fun every so often might be good."

"Competing *is* fun," I argued. "I know you're not that bothered but you like riding, don't you? Riding's fun."

"Definitely," she agreed. "But sometimes a change is good too. More relaxed riding, maybe. I mean you can't top today, can you? You and Scarlet won every class you entered, you got the most points for the team and I bet everyone's still talking about that awesome last show jumping round."

"It was great." I wasn't boasting, just re-living the sensation of Scarlet's final turn, the way she'd swiveled almost at right angles to fly like a gleaming fiery arrow into a perfect take-off, soaring over the last jump and galloping to victory. "But look, Luce, if you're fed up with hanging around all the shows –"

"No, I like it, honest," she said, securing the last of Scarlet's travel boots. "I was just hoping you wouldn't want to be doing it all the time, that's all."

I looked at her curiously. I really like Lucy, despite the fact she's almost exactly my opposite in every way. I'm tall and dark, she's blonde and tiny. I'm loud and bossy, she's quiet and sweet – the list goes on but we get along fantastically well and are very best friends. She owns a pretty skewbald pony named Petal who is as unlike my Scarlet as you can get, but it doesn't seem to bother them either, and the four of us spend a lot of time together. Lucy and Petal like mounted games and a little jumping but they don't have any ambitions to belong to our club competition team. They're great fans though, and Lucy is just the best supporter I could wish for, not only turning up to cheer me on at every show but helping out as groom/friend/cheer-leader/commiserating-chocolate-provider in whatever order was needed! Now, though, she was looking as though she could do with a buddy herself.

"It doesn't need to be *every* day," I assured her. "I mean, I'll still go shopping in town, or whatever other stuff you want to do."

"It's more than that," Lucy gave her last polo mint to

7

Scarlet. "In fact – oh I don't know, Dana – seeing what you were like today I can't possibly ask."

"Sure you can," I encouraged her. "We're best buds, aren't we?"

"Well," she said reluctantly. "There's some sort of crisis in our family, an old uncle who's got problems, and Mom and Dad want to go and help. I'd have to go too, but they said there's plenty of room, land and everything, so I can take Petal and they thought maybe you and Scarlet would come with us?"

This all came out in a rush as though she'd practiced saying it a lot.

"Don't look so worried," I gave her a hug. "Where is this place?"

"Up north somewhere," she waved a hand vaguely. "I've never been, but it's a big old house on the edge of a wild prairie."

"Sounds like great riding country," I gave my pony's back one last rub. "Count us in."

"Oh *thanks,* Dana," her face shone with relief. "The trouble is my parents are going to be involved with this uncle all day so they won't have time to ferry us around, which means no shows for you and Scarlet."

"No problem." To be honest, I did feel that part was a real pain, but even if Scarlet and I were in for a non-competitive couple of weeks, I was happy to say yes and support my friend.

"I hope it's not going to be too low-key for you, Dana," Joe, Lucy's dad said, seeming quite concerned when I went over to their house to get the details. "I know what a live wire you are, and from what I remember about staying at

8

Uncle James's place when I was a kid – well, it's pretty quiet, to say the least."

"It'll be fine," I assured him. "Lucy says the house is right on the edge of some wild prairie land so we'll have a lot of fun up there with the horses."

"Well, yes it is," he looked even more worried. "But the prairie's a bit *too* wild for you to just take off across it."

"You mean it's *dangerous*?" Lucy squealed. "You didn't say anything about dangerous, Dad."

"The part near the house is OK," Joe said defensively. "I used to ride my bike up there, but everyone said it was risky and warned not to go too far and to stay on the trails."

I looked at my friend's horrified face and my heart sank. Lucy's great, but she wasn't in the line when the word *adventurous* was handed out.

"It's probably safer now," I said encouragingly. "If you haven't been back since you were a kid, Joe, it will probably have changed a lot."

"Maybe, though the only difference I saw in the area when I last visited my uncle was that the little town a few miles away had grown into a bigger town."

"When was that?" Lucy asked curiously. "I thought you hadn't seen this Uncle James for years and years. You've never taken *me* to see him before, I know that."

"That's right," her Mom, Molly, said quietly. "I've actually only met him twice myself – he's never been exactly sociable."

"Sounds like it," Lucy grumbled. "If he's never even bothered to invite me and Ty up to his spooky old house."

Ty's her older brother. He's off traveling, taking a year off before college.

"My uncle *has* seen Ty, but not since he was a baby,"

9

Joe said carefully, reluctant to elaborate. "There was a –
falling out – between Uncle James and me, and we haven't
seen or spoken to him for nearly fifteen years."

"Since I was born, in fact," Lucy was sounding more and
more aggrieved while I found myself wishing quite seriously
that I hadn't agreed to join in this weird family reunion. The
vacation was sounding more dire by the minute – a gloomy
old house in the middle of nowhere, an Uncle who sounded
like a total misery, countryside unsuitable for riding, no
horse shows, no friends to hang out with – there didn't seem
to be one reason to go along. I was actually on the point of
opening my mouth and making some kind of excuse when
Lucy turned a sad face toward me and said fervently, "I'm
really glad you're going to be with me, Dana. I just don't
know what I'd do there without you."

"Oh, I'm sure it will be cool," I said, trying to sound as
if I meant it. "We'll find stuff to do and your uncle's bound
to like you once you meet."

"Sounds like it!" She glared at her parents. "Like he was
so thrilled when I was born he never invited us back to his
rotten old house."

"Oh Lucy," her dad sighed. "It's more complicated than
that. I'll tell you the whole story one day, but all you need to
know now is that Uncle James is an old man who needs help.
And we're family and that's what families do – they help."

Put like that there wasn't much else my friend could
say, but I knew, like me, she wasn't looking forward to
spending two precious weeks of the school vacation in
what we privately referred to as Spooksville Hall. Its actual
name was Cornell Hall, and it was situated, Joe told us,
about four miles from the little town of Cornell.

❖ ❖ ❖ ❖ ❖

"That sign says *Welcome to Cornell*," I announced. It was two weeks later and Lucy and I were in the back of the car, with me keeping a close eye on the trailer containing Scarlet and Petal. "It's tiny, you said, right?"

"It certainly was when I was a kid, and still pretty small fifteen years ago." Joe, driving with extra care because of the horse trailer, was looking surprised. "But it's grown a lot. The big estate on our right wasn't here last time I drove through."

We looked out at the huddle of houses that gradually thinned as we went deeper into the countryside.

"That's attractive," Molly said, pointing to a white-fronted house standing in the middle of a big garden. "Oh look girls, horses!"

We'd already spotted the posh paddocks, the schooling ring set up with colored jumps and the ponies grazing in the distance.

"Very nice," Lucy said approvingly. "Is it close enough to Uncle James's place for us to ride over and say hello?"

"You mean *hello, can we use your jumps?*" I joked, having perked up a lot.

"I reckon it is," Joe said, turning the car carefully to drive along a narrower road. "Cornell Hall's only a mile or so down here."

"Great!" I bounced around excitedly. "See Lucy, I told you it was going to be OK."

"Don't talk too soon," she warned. "We haven't seen where we're staying yet."

Filled with excitement I was sure Uncle James's house would be nothing like we'd imagined, but probably a nice, normal place with a pretty garden and –

"Oh Dana," Lucy said, clutching my arm, "There it is!"

11

Even from a distance you could see Cornell Hall was crumbling, with discolored bricks, peeling paint and rotting timbers. Its roof sagged low over jutting eaves as though the neglected house was frowning at the world beyond the tangle of trees crowding in on it.

"Ugh!" Lucy's pretty face was a picture of distaste. "It looks like something from a horror movie, like it's crouching there ready to pounce."

"Don't be silly," Molly said sharply, but I thought she looked pretty shaken herself. "It's just in need of some TLC, that's all."

"And a few thousand dollars spent on it," Joe said with feeling. "Uncle James was always pretty careful with his money, but from the look of things he hasn't even forked out for basic maintenance."

He'd stopped the car outside rusty iron gates where a sign reading *Cornell Hall* was so moss covered and dirty, it was almost illegible.

"What if the gates are locked?" Lucy asked nervously. "Or what if they're not and there are dogs? Fierce dogs?"

"Your Uncle doesn't like dogs," Joe said, getting out of the car.

The gates creaked and groaned theatrically when he pushed them open, and the house only needed a crash of thunder and some forked lightning to perfect the Dracula's Castle impression. Thankfully the sun was shining from a cloudless blue sky, but you'd hardly have known it from the faded front door. Dark, heavy fir trees towered above us, blocking out most of the light as their dense branches formed a canopy over and around the house. I saw Lucy shiver and patted her arm comfortingly.

12

"It'll be warmer inside."

"I'm not cold, I'm spooked." She huddled against me, watching her parents approach the front door. "It's even worse than I thought. We can't stay here, Dana."

"Sure we can," I refused to be downhearted. "It'll be – um – an adventure. Come on, let's get the horses out."

I jumped out of the car and ran over to the trailer. Scarlet isn't the best traveler in the world and gets very anxious once we stop, so I wanted to unload her before she got too wound up. The latch on Lucy's trailer is quite stiff so I was struggling to undo it when a gruff voice said disapprovingly, "You look more like a boy than a girl with that hair and those pants."

I wear my naturally curly dark hair short and spiky but it suits me, and I've been told my long legs look good in jeans, so I was naturally a bit offended.

"Well I'm not," I carried on fiddling with the lock. "You must be Mr. – um – Harmon. I'm Dana."

"Oh, you're the other one," the old man said. He reached up and slid the latch and I looked him directly in the eye.

He was very old, with crumpled leathery skin and white hair. Unlike the house, he looked clean and cared for, but his bristling eyebrows were drawn together over angry, faded blue eyes in almost exactly the same frown as the sagging roof.

He doesn't want us in his house any more than we want to be here, I thought and was about to turn away when I saw his brows lift and the bad tempered, scornful expression turn for an instant to one of joyful recognition.

"You're – you're –" he was staring at my friend.

"Lucy Harmon," she put out a small hand. "And you're Uncle James. My mom and dad have been ringing your door bell."

14

"It doesn't work, which suits me fine because I never have visitors and don't want them either. Anyway, Kay's in the garden and Mervyn can't manage the front hall," he shook his head as if to clear it. "I suppose I'm stuck with having you here, so I'll go and see them while you get on with setting up your horses."

"Duh!" Lucy sounded really aggrieved as she watched him stomp away. "That went well, didn't it! Dad warned me my uncle was a grouch but I thought he'd at least be polite!"

"He wasn't too bad with you. In fact he definitely softened when you turned up. He'd already looked at me like I'd crawled out from under a rock, and said I was more like a boy than a girl."

"Charming!" Lucy strode crossly up the trailer's ramp and untied her pony. "If he's always that rude Dad might just as well turn the car around and head for home now."

"Oh, your uncle will ease up," I tried to cheer her. "And if not, we'll keep out of his way by spending all day with the horses." I was checking Scarlet over carefully, pleased that she'd only sweated a little and seemed absolutely fine. "Lucy, I hope the paddocks are in better shape than the house. We can't put these two in some ramshackle old field."

"Don't worry, I checked. Dad says a neighboring farmer's been renting some grazing land for years and has maintained it well."

"Great, as long as it's not full of sheep or cows!" I joked, following her across the weedy drive, leading my pony who was looking around with interest.

"It isn't," she answered seriously. "One of the problems we're here to sort out is that Uncle James has had a huge quarrel with the neighbor over some boundary dispute so the farm livestock aren't here right now." She pointed ahead, "That must be the field, Dana."

I was relieved to see a well-fenced paddock complete with water trough, and took Scarlet through its heavy metal gate feeling much happier. It wasn't huge but the grazing looked good, so, having scanned the neat post and rail fence to make sure it was secure, we took off the ponies' head collars and let them explore their vacation home. I love watching horses when they're introduced to new surroundings. Our two took off immediately, nostrils flaring with excitement as they cantered to the far side of the field. Scarlet, her mane and tail streaming like red-gold silk ribbons, sailed into an extended trot, covering the ground in a glorious long-striding rhythm while the skewbald Petal pounded less elegantly alongside.

"Petal looks like a little round bridesmaid following a perfect, slender bride," Lucy laughed affectionately. "Oh, look at Scarlet now!"

My pony had stopped suddenly, arching her neck playfully, then spun in a perfect forehand turn to canter back toward us, throwing her hind legs up in a series of high, exuberant bucks. Petal shook her white and tan head as if to say, "Too much for me!"

"That's enough excitement for my girl," Lucy watched fondly as her pony slowed to a halt. "She'll get right down to some serious grazing now!"

Scarlet carried on for a little longer, moving with the kind of grace and poetry horses can produce so easily when they're not impeded by a rider, till at last she sank to the ground and had a good roll, squirming ecstatically against the strong green grass below her. I was so pleased to see her enjoying herself that the prospect of two weeks in

Spooksville Hall with Uncle Grumpy hardly bothered me at all. It was still bugging Lucy though.

"I hope Dad's had a firm word with Uncle James about the way he needs to treat us," she said as she clambered over the gate and jumped down. "We came here to help, so the least he can do is be pleasant."

Pleasant, however, was not the word I'd use to describe the scene back at the house. The front door had been left open so after some knocking and polite, "Hello, may we come in?" calling, we ventured inside. The hall was narrow and very dark with several doors leading from it, but we knew exactly where to find Lucy's family simply by following the noise. Uncle James was in full flow, his creaky old voice gaining surprising volume as he carried on roaring.

"I'm supposed to be grateful, am I? Just because a few problems were mentioned you think you can turn up here and take over the place! Telling me what to do and how to spend my money! It's the money you're interested in, I suppose – is that why you're really here?"

"No it is not!" Joe's voice was quieter but just as vehement. "I told you on the phone, Uncle James, we're just here to help. Your neighbor, Mr. Barlow, contacted us first, worried that things were getting too much for you, and –"

"Interfering old busybody! He's only thinking of himself and the cheap grazing I let him have. I suppose he gave you my number, because I certainly didn't, and it's not in the book."

"Joe explained to him that we'd like to come up and sort things out," Molly said, trying to calm him. "We're concerned about you, Uncle James."

"You can all just pack up your concern and take it back home. I don't want it!"

The old man stamped angrily out of the room, brushing past Lucy and me without a word or even a glance. I took one look at the faces of my friend and her parents and thought philosophically, *Oh well, Scarlet's enjoyed a good twenty minutes of the vacation but I think she'll be back in the trailer any time now!*

Chapter TWO

I'm absolutely sure Joe was just about to open his mouth and tell us the visit was over when a thin, reedy voice from the other side of the room cut in.

"Oh dear, what a shame. And you were hoping the old boy would welcome you with open arms, I expect?"

Curious, I stepped forward and saw a wheelchair at the open door opposite where we were standing. The man in it smiled.

"Oh you're the great-niece, are you? Not much family resemblance, I'd say."

"That's because I'm not related," I said shortly. "I'm Lucy's friend – Mr. Harmon's *her* uncle."

"Pleased to meet you, if only briefly. I'm Mervyn," he said, and maneuvered the chair clumsily to face us in the narrow doorway. "My wife and I have looked after the old gentleman for some years now. Obviously the last few months have proved difficult, but we're hoping to be back to normal soon."

Joe, still looking shell-shocked after his uncle's diatribe, shook Mervyn's hand politely. "I heard you had an accident – a car crash, was it?"

"Yes, a car, anyway. As you see at the moment I'm confined to this chair and it's curtailed the carrying out of my usual duties. There's no need to worry though, so feel free to leave Mr. Harmon to our care. As soon as I'm up and about I'll get back to work."

"That's good news but, well, without wishing to be rude, I do feel the repairs required around the house and grounds need a professional builder," Joe said, standing stiffly, his body language screaming that he'd rather be anywhere doing anything other than having this conversation.

"No, no," Mervyn shook his head with maddening complacency. "You don't know our old gentleman at all. He's careful with the pennies, you see, and doesn't like to spend them unnecessarily."

"I think it is very necessary to keep the peace with the neighboring farmer," Joe retorted sharply. "Mr. Barlow has had a good working relationship with my uncle for years but now the state of the boundary fences make it impossible to keep his animals safe."

"Money again. Farmer Barlow expected Mr. Harmon to pay half the costs."

"Perfectly reasonable, especially as Barlow's kept the pastures he rents in good order, at his own expense. Anyway," Joe pulled himself up with an effort. "I shouldn't be discussing this with you, should I? I'm sure my uncle –"

"He won't change his mind," Mervyn had an irritatingly smug way of saying things. "Stubborn as a mule, he is."

"You think so?" There was a glint in Joe's eye I'd never seen before. "It must be something that runs in the family then, because I don't give up easily either. Could you tell us where we'll be sleeping, please Mervyn? I'll get our bags so we can all unpack."

The look of surprise he got from the man in the wheelchair was nothing to the expression of outraged disbelief etched on Lucy's face.

"Dad!" she caught up with him outside the front door. "What are you doing? We can't stay here after the way Uncle James spoke to you. *He* doesn't want us here and *we* don't want to stay, so why are we unpacking?"

"Look, I've made the effort to come here and I'm not being chased off by my uncle's – uh – show of irritation."

"Irritation?" Molly still looked pretty shaken. "I'd use a stronger word to describe it. Lucy's right, Joe, your uncle's made it clear he doesn't want our help."

"You think I should abandon him to Mervyn's shoddy ministrations?" Joe was shaking with suppressed anger. "Most of the problems here are caused by neglect and mismanagement, and a lot of that comes down to the way Mervyn has consistently botched the work that needs to be done."

"Duh! So you're making us stay in this ghastly old place just because you took a dislike to Mervyn?" Lucy, quiet, gentle Lucy was nearly as furious as her father. "Terrific, thanks, Dad!"

He stopped, his hand on the trunk of the car, his head bowed. "If you're really unhappy you and Dana can go home. I *have* to stay."

"You mean you'd let me drive the girls and the ponies away and leave you here?" Molly put her arms around him and he raised his head to look at her. "No way, Joe – if you're staying we're all staying."

I heard a sharp intake of breath from my friend and nudged her quickly.

"You have to back them up, Lucy," I said quietly. "It'll be all right. We're going to spend all our time out with the horses, remember?"

"I don't get it," she said loudly. "But if that's what you two want then we'll stay too, but I'm not promising to be nice."

"You're always nice," Joe's shoulders relaxed and he

21

even managed a smile. "You'll have your Great-Uncle James eating out of your hand within a day or two."

"Yuk!" Lucy reached over and took her bag. "What a horrible thought. Come on, Dana, let's go and see what sort of disgusting room they've given us to sleep in."

To our surprise though, the bedroom under the sagging eaves was OK. It was a little dark and old fashioned but scrupulously clean and it even had its own bathroom.

"I have never seen plumbing like that before," Lucy surveyed the huge, cumbersome bath and sink, "but as long as it works I guess it's all right."

"It's fine," I said, peering out of the window. "And if some of these trees were cut down we could see into the paddock."

"I'll ask Dad to see to it while he's putting everything else right. You know, I've never seen him as mad as he was just now, Dana. He didn't like Uncle James going off at him, but it was Mervyn who really got under his skin."

"I don't think it was a personal thing," I said slowly. "It's the whole scenario. Your dad's shocked at the level of neglect and probably found Mervyn's smug acceptance of it too much to take."

"Oh, don't go all deep and meaningful on me! I'm just going to stay out of it," Lucy stowed her empty bag on top of the wardrobe. "Let's go and explore, OK?"

"Indoors or out?" I asked.

"Out first. I don't want dear Uncle James leaping out at us in one of these narrow corridors."

"That's what he must have meant when he said Mervyn couldn't manage the front hall," I realized. "You wouldn't get a wheelchair around those tight corners."

"Mm, makes you wonder why a mean and grumpy old

man like my uncle would keep employing a handy man who's no longer handy, doesn't it?" Lucy shook her head. "Still, like I said, I don't want to get involved. Where shall we start our exploring?"

"Follow me," I said confidently. "We'll start at the paddock and work our way around."

It took a while because as well as the big, overgrown gardens, there were two more fields, both neatly fenced but completely empty.

"More of Farmer Barlow's work," I said, patting a sturdy post appreciatively. "I wonder which boundary line they're having the argument about."

Lucy opened her mouth to say, *who cares,* but I threw a handful of grass in her face, making her cough and splutter instead.

She retaliated by filling a bucket from a water trough and chasing me with it until I hid behind a tree and tripped her. We felt better after this childish burst of energy, and when we reached a particularly inviting old oak tree I suggested we climb up to inspect the view. It was difficult picturing the overall scene from the ground with its dense swathes of undergrowth and scrubby patches of self-sown saplings. The oak tree made a good vantage point from halfway up and we leaned against its gnarled trunk and looked across the landscape. From here you could see most of the shaggy, unkempt grass that used to be a lawn and part of a rickety line of leaning posts and sagging wire bordering yet another empty field.

"That must be the fence that caused the falling out between the farmer and your uncle," I told Lucy, but she was still doing her *don't talk to me about him* act, so I shinned further up the tree to find out what else I could see.

"Ooh, look, Lucy!" I said and pointed in excitement. "There's the prairie – the wild and mysterious prairie – it looks beautiful!"

"Yeah?" Lucy tried to reach up. "I can't get any higher. It's all right for you, climbing around like a long legged monkey."

"Charming! I wish you and your family would say something nice about me for a change."

"It was meant as a compliment," she said, and gritted her teeth and tried to climb again. "No, I can't do it."

"Shuffle along to the end of the branch," I encouraged her.

"I'm too scared. Describe the prairie to me instead."

"It looks kind of bleak," I scanned the distance obligingly. "A sort of rolling expanse of brownish green with a few blobs of color – purple and bright yellow."

"That'll be wildflowers," she said knowledgeably. "Is it hilly?"

"The bit I can see is flattish," I struggled to get even higher. "Oh, there's a big black looking hill and – ooh, someone's up there! I can see a tiny figure and something flashing in the sunlight – he must be using binoculars."

"I hope he's not spying on us," Lucy said severely. "This is Harmon land, it's private."

"Listen to you!" I grinned down at her. "All of a sudden you're Lady Harmon of Cornell Hall!"

"Yeah, well," she started clambering cautiously back down. "No one likes a nosy neighbor."

"Oh, you think it's the farmer?" I slid easily down to join her. "So where's the Barlow farmhouse? I couldn't see any other buildings nearby."

"It's over to the west somewhere. Mr. Barlow doesn't

have much grazing land, my dad says, because the natural terrain's just prairie."

"I liked the look of that prairie," I said, enthusiastically. "Shall we take the horses up there later?"

"I could ask Dad to show us the way if he can borrow a bike."

Personally I'd prefer to go on a riding exploration without a guide but although Lucy had regained her usual sweet temper, she still seemed a bit touchy so I didn't object. I was hungry by now and wondered whether we'd have to go into town for some lunch, but Molly came out to find us and said Kay had prepared something.

"Kay is Mervyn's wife, isn't she?" Lucy looked reluctant. "What's she like?"

"She seems very nice," Molly said firmly. "Extremely quiet, but she's a good cook and she keeps that scruffy old house incredibly clean. Your dad's already told her he's very grateful."

"Yeah, whatever," Lucy was overdoing the *don't talk to me about the situation* attitude, I thought.

We followed Molly into a kitchen that looked as though it had stepped straight out of a history book. I don't mean medieval, more sort of 1950's with gingham curtains, a scrubbed wood table and a sink. There wasn't a fitted cupboard in sight, just a big dresser with plates and cups on display and a heavy, range-type stove. I'd been dreading having to sit and make polite conversation with Uncle James or Mervyn, so I was relieved to find only Joe and a small mousey-looking woman who gave us a brief, tight-lipped smile before setting a dish of something wonderful smelling on the table.

"Hi girls," Joe sounded determinedly cheerful. "It's just us four this lunch time, apparently. Everyone else is – um – busy, isn't that right, Kay?"

"Yes," she had a strangely colorless voice. "Mr. Harmon likes to eat alone when he's doing his office work but I dare say you'll see him at dinner. There's just soup and crusty bread now, will that do?"

"It smells great," Lucy said politely. "I'm Lucy and this is my friend Dana."

"Kay. How do you do," she barely made eye contact before sliding noiselessly out of the room.

"Spooky woman," Lucy remarked, sniffing at her soup.

"But as you said, Molly, she can cook all right," I said. Like Joe, I was determined to be upbeat.

The homemade soup and bread were delicious, though being more used to burger-type snacks, I felt even more that we were vacationing in a time warp.

"We're going to ride this afternoon," Lucy told her parents. "That's OK, isn't it? I mean, we don't have to help here or anything, do we?"

"No, you're fine," Joe said absently. "We're still at the negotiating stage, trying to convince Uncle James."

"Good luck with that," Lucy said with feeling, turning back to me. "You want to take the horses up to the prairie, don't you, Dana?"

"Oh I don't think that's a good idea," Molly looked worried. "I think you should wait for someone to go with you. The prairie seems to have quite a reputation."

"That's true," Lucy said. She's easily dissuaded. "We'll just wander over to the lanes instead. I know – we can pay a visit to that white house we saw."

"OK," I agreed amiably. "But from what I saw of it I'd really like to try the prairie soon."

"I'll see what I can do," Joe promised. "Just give me time to work on my uncle so we can get this boundary issue resolved at the very least."

"Oh sure." I finished my soup. "That was yummy."

Kay had also left a big bowl of fresh raspberries and some cream, and despite being a bit disappointed about the afternoon's ride I was feeling more optimistic about our stay at Cornell Hall. Without Uncle James and Mervyn winding anyone up it was perfectly pleasant, and it seemed the food was going to be five-star standard. The main problem, as far as I could see, would be boredom brought on by a lack of exciting riding and interesting people. I'd have to work on my friend to get a decent ride on the prairie, but in the meantime would have to be content with a tame saunter around the quiet lanes surrounding the house. Being used to having a stable yard, I felt odd getting the horses ready outdoors, but they didn't seem to mind and Scarlet, as always, was very enthusiastic about going out.

"She's going to be disappointed with this short jaunt," Lucy said apologetically. "*You* don't mind, do you, Dana?"

"Course not," I lied. "Let's try that white house first, OK? You never know, we might get invited in."

The fashionable paddocks, when we reached them, however, were unoccupied, but after a long inspection of the schooling ring and jumps, I pointed to a narrow trail leading away from the road along the perimeter fence.

"Let's try up there."

"Do you think?" Lucy looked worried. "Maybe it's private – I think we should stick to the road."

"Nah. The horses will be bored if we do that. There aren't any *Keep Out* signs, and I think the trail leads to the woods you can see behind the house."

"If someone comes out and chases us off it'll be your fault," Lucy grumbled, but she turned Petal to follow me.

The first part of the trail ran alongside the schooling ring and wasn't that well defined. In fact Scarlet had to push her way through overhanging branches a few times, but although I could hear my friend moaning I kept going. We were now passing a harrowed and re-seeded paddock and at the far end of it I spotted a gate leading out to the trail which now widened considerably.

"Look," I turned to Lucy. "The people who live here must use this route a lot, and I was right, it does lead up to the woods which means there's probably a decent ride for us."

"As long as we're not trespassing," she was still worrying. "I suppose you noticed the horses we saw earlier are gone from their field now?"

"Yeah, and I'm hoping we'll meet up with their riders. They'll be able to show us around," I moved Scarlet into a trot, eager to see what lay ahead.

At the top of the slope the path wound its way into a shady wood, full of filtered sunshine and birdsong. We cantered along a short stretch, taking two small jumps built from fallen branches. I was already approving of the people who rode here. Their well-kept fields were impressive and they obviously made the most of their rides out. The woods, though pretty and very pleasant to ride through weren't that exciting, and I really hoped the trail would take us to something a little more out of the ordinary. A sudden clearing gave us another chance for a brief canter and I was delighted to find a broad, shallow stream bordering the next clump of trees. Scarlet cleared it effortlessly, picking up beautifully to canter smoothly away. I had to laugh when I turned to watch Lucy. She and Petal were paddling through, the skewbald pony picking her way daintily across the cool, clear water.

"That's cheating!" I called out sternly. "You're supposed to jump it."

"There's no rule that says so," Lucy said, reasonably enough. "Stop acting like a school teacher. We're not in a hurry anyway."

"I guess that's true," I sighed inwardly and waited for them to catch up. "But wouldn't it be more fun if we pretended we were trying to win a top competition or something?"

"No," she said firmly. "I'm just enjoying being in the countryside on a lovely day. Your trouble is you're always looking for excitement and life's just not like that!"

I supposed she was right and had to remind myself I'd accepted that these two weeks were going to be a lot more sedate than Scarlet and I were used to. I was here to support Lucy and her family, so I told myself I must curb what everyone tells me is a highly-developed spirit of adventure and live in the real world for once. It was at that exact moment that Scarlet and I emerged from a belt of trees onto another much larger clearing. There, straight ahead, was a stunning white horse being ridden flat out in competition style through a cross-country course by the best looking rider I'd ever seen in my life!

Chapter THREE

I honestly thought all my Christmases and birthdays had come at once, when from behind me Lucy said loudly, "Who's that?"

I had to stop myself from answering dreamily. *I don't know, but he's wonderful,* when, at the sound of her voice the rider shot a startled glance in our direction, losing both balance and concentration so that the stunning white horse ducked immediately to one side of the log pile they were approaching and dumped him unceremoniously before cantering wildly away. Without hesitation I shot forward, galloping Scarlet across the clearing at an angle to catch the bolting horse before he could go charging into the next bank of trees. Bringing my pony alongside it, I leaned over and grabbed the loose reins, checking both horses and bringing them smoothly down through their paces to halt. The big white horse's sides were heaving and I spoke to him quietly, soothing his nervous trembling and letting him lean his nose into Scarlet's side to calm him. By the time I'd walked them both across the clearing to the line of jumps, his rider was on his feet, and had brushed himself off. Despite seeming deeply self-conscious and annoyed with himself, he looked up and smiled straight into my eyes. Honestly, it was such a knee-buckling, fantastic moment I nearly fell off my own horse and let the gorgeous white one go again.

"Hi," I tried to be cool and failed dismally. "Um – here's your horse."

I handed him the reins and he stroked the silky white neck ruefully. "Thanks a lot. I'd like to say that very rarely happens but I'd be lying, I'm afraid."

31

"Oh, my brother's not *that* bad," a girl on a chunky bay cob said as she arrived with Lucy behind her and grinned at me. "Polar only throws a wobbly three or four times a week."

"You're kidding!" Lucy looked horrified. "I felt so guilty at startling you like that, but I didn't realize you fall off so often."

"I don't always fall off." Sounding defensive, the boy climbed stiffly into the white horse's saddle. "But when I do, Page has never been able to catch Polar the way your friend did – um, sorry, I didn't get your name?"

"Dana," I said, still trying to get my breath back after that smile. "And this is Lucy."

"I'm Evan and I'm really pleased to meet you, even though I haven't made *that* great a first impression!"

If you only knew! I thought silently.

"Evan's training in the hope of being selected for our Pony Club Competition Squad," Page said chattily. "Are you into cross-country, show jumping and all that stuff, Lucy?"

"Not me," she looked horrified at the thought. "Petal and I enjoy the occasional flag race and we usually try for a rosette in the clear-round jumping ring at the show ground, but we leave the real thing to Dana and Scarlet."

"Who are, if that bit of rescue riding is anything to go by, a couple of stars," Evan said. Still seeming embarrassed, he sounded a little awkward, but his white teeth shone in his tanned face.

Are you getting the picture here? Yeah, you're right, I was totally, utterly knocked out by him.

"You're right about Scarlet, but I'm nothing special," I said, hoping I sounded suitably modest. "But I don't mind giving you some help with the selection training if you want."

32

"You mean you live around here?" The excitement in his voice made my insides go into meltdown again.

"Just for a couple of weeks. We're staying with Lucy's uncle at Spooks – I mean Cornell Hall."

"No way! No one ever visits the Hall," Page looked at Lucy in surprise. "I didn't even know the old man had any family."

"Uncle James came as something of a shock to me too," Lucy said ruefully. "So – well, we're hoping to spend most of our time here out with the horses."

"We were looking for somewhere interesting to ride," I explained. "And we followed that trail by the white house."

"That's where we live," Evan said, riding very close to me. "Maybe you noticed Polar and Blade in the paddock when you drove past?"

I nodded, praying that Lucy wouldn't chime in and tell him we'd been hoping for an invitation to use their ring.

"How come you didn't go straight up to the prairie?" Page asked Lucy. "It's just behind your uncle's place."

"My dad said we shouldn't go there without a guide."

"Well now you have one, in fact you've got two." Evan was smiling at me again. "Unless you'd rather just amble around here?"

"Dana doesn't do ambling," Lucy said darkly. "Petal and I don't mind it at all, but she and Scarlet are always galloping and jumping all over the place, pretending –"

"I think that's a *yes please, we'd love you to show us the prairie*," I broke in hastily. I didn't want Evan to think I was some kind of fanatic, playing at being in a competition all the time. "Do we have to go back to the road first?"

"No, we can get through from the end of these woods," Page said, turning Blade and pointing ahead.

My sense of direction's not that strong and I was surprised when, after a fairly short trek through the trees, we came out into a clearing and there, to our left, was the hunched mass of Cornell Hall. The broad, sandy trail we were now on wound uphill, through another smaller wooded area and then, as we emerged from that, the prairie spread before us. We have nice riding country at home, but it's comparatively tame, with pretty, grassy meadows and gentle riversides, so the sudden, stark expanse of scrubby heather and bracken rolling into the distance was a shock. The soil was thin and sandy, and in places great chunks of rock reared up as though the bones of the earth itself were showing through. The dark, humped shape of the hill I'd seen from my treetop perch loomed just ahead with the occasional blaze of color dotted around it. Bees buzzed in a purple patch nearby and, despite there being only the occasional stunted tree, I could hear a bird singing.

"Mm," Lucy said, "Dramatic! It's all right on a day like this, but I wouldn't want to be up here in a storm."

"I think the prairie would look fantastic whatever the weather," I disagreed, and Evan gave me his great smile.

"We like it, but Lucy's dad is right. Parts of it are treacherous, so we tend to stay around this area."

"Really?" I knew I'd be itching to explore further afield if I lived here. Right now, though, I was longing to gallop and I could feel Scarlet, who obviously felt the same, begin to prance with eagerness beneath me. "OK, show us where!"

"Fast or slow?" he asked and laughed aloud when I

34

immediately responded, "Fast!" at the same time as Lucy said, "Slow please."

"We can do both," Page said amicably. "Lucy and I will do the quiet part and catch up with you two if you like."

I saw the glint in Evan's eyes as he put his showy, powerful horse into a canter and I joined him at once, my pony moving easily to match his stride.

"We'll gallop up there," Evan pointed ahead where the sandy trail sloped gradually away.

It was the perfect place to let Scarlet go, and I felt her lengthen into the classic four-time beat, each stride covering the maximum amount of ground with a flowing, glorious sense of speed. Evan, after a startled glance at us, kept alongside with Polar showing no sign of getting ahead, and we zoomed along the uphill trail as though we were joined together in a red and white streak. I felt, as always, like a bird in flight, skimming over the ground in an explosion of power and grace. Evan said something but his words were carried away on the warm summer wind and I shook my head, wondering what romantic phrase he was using to describe how he felt.

"I said," he roared loudly. "I can't believe that little mare's so fast! I'm going to slow down now, OK?"

Our downward transition, I have to say, was smoother than his, and Scarlet was hardly blowing at all when we halted, unlike Polar whose sides were heaving from the exertion.

"Who are you calling a little mare?" I enquired flippantly and Evan turned a worried, though still cute, face toward me.

"Not you – your horse obviously. I mean, she's not that big, and yet Polar could only just keep up with her pace."

35

"It's fitness that counts," I said smugly. "We're in better condition than you two."

He gave me an admiring look from those brilliant blue eyes. "You do look good, I'll give you that."

"Thank you, kind sir," I said, thinking that clowning around was a lot cooler than showing how happy he made me feel. "Are there any jumps up here?"

"A few banks and ditches, that's all. We haven't tried building a course because Polar gets jittery on the prairie. Still," he gave me that look again, "we've set up those jumps in the clearing so you could always come over and use those."

"Yeah, they look good," I said. "OK, thanks and – um – in return, as I said, I'll be glad to help with your training."

"Yeah?" he said hopefully. "That would be great, but you're sure it won't take up too much of your vacation time?"

"Oh, I don't mind," I said airily. "Cornell Hall is a good place to be out of, if you get my meaning. I really love competition work and so does Scarlet, and Lucy's already said she wants to spend as much time as possible out riding, so we'll all be happy."

"I'll be more than happy, I'll be –" Words seemed to fail him.

"Thanks for waiting!" Lucy and Page finally caught up with us.

"It's OK," I said dreamily, my mind full of long, exciting training sessions with Evan, which meant hours of togetherness where we grew closer and closer. It was such a lovely picture I hardly noticed where we were going or what I was doing.

Scarlet helped by giving one of her exuberant bucks,

nearly throwing me out of the saddle, which I thought could be her way of telling me to concentrate.

"Where shall we go now?" I looked around at the unfamiliar terrain. "How about over there? I can see splashes of green, so if that's grass we could maybe have a race."

"Not a good idea," Evan's face was serious. "That area is totally boggy and the greenish bits you can see are marsh plants growing over the mud."

"You mean mud like quicksand?" Lucy's eyes were round. "If we rode over there the ponies would just sink into the ground and disappear?"

"They'd certainly sink," Evan said with feeling. "I fell off my bike over there when I was a kid and went waist deep before I got hauled out."

"And the trails aren't well defined so they're not easy to follow," Page said, shaking back her long braid. "So the answer is no, even for a daredevil like you, Dana."

"We'll canter along the main trail as far as Jagged Tor, where you'll get a pretty good view of the safe places to ride." Evan's face, grim when he spoke about the marsh, was warm as he smiled at me.

There was no need for them both, I thought, to talk to me as if I was some kind of maniac just because I like a little excitement in my riding. I'd never put Scarlet in that kind of danger so I was happy to canter well away from the murky marshes.

We could see the huge elevated rock called Jagged Tor long before we reached it, and when we finally came to a halt beside its towering, slate-gray mass, both Lucy and I gasped at the vista around us. In every direction the prairie rolled into the distance, a huge, wild expanse of brooding brown and gray. To the north were darker patches with a covering of the acid green I'd noticed before.

"That whole area is dangerous," Evan leaned across his horse to point. He was so close I could smell the clean, outdoorsy smell of his skin.

I nodded seriously, "So although there *are* trails, we just stay away from there?"

"It's possible to get across, of course, but you see those faint lines that sort of break up here and there? That's the sandy trail that runs through it, and it's so narrow and convoluted it's just not the best place to ride. Polar absolutely hates it, so, as I say, we tend to avoid it. Anyway, even if you're clever enough not to sink in one of the marshy bogs it's not much fun, whereas this way –" he turned slightly so that our faces were now almost touching, "Is terrific."

"Terrific," I said faintly, feeling my insides bouncing like I was on a trampoline.

"Where's Cornell Hall from here?" Lucy didn't seem to notice I'd practically lost the power of speech. "We've ridden in a rough semi-circle, so are we heading back toward it now?"

"Very good," Page said admiringly. "Most people completely lose their bearings out here."

I felt very decidedly that I was one of those people, but I put it down more to being in touching distance of Evan than my normal lack of any sense of direction.

"There are some banks and a ditch or two over by the lightning tree," Evan said, looking slightly worried again. "I know you're dying to do some jumping so we'll do those on the ride home, OK?"

"Sure," I said, taking a while to recover from the physical nearness of him. "Scarlet will like that."

The trail had widened, its broad, sandy surface perfect for another canter which we did in a line of four, keeping the horses together like a precision cavalry troop. Scarlet got very excited, pulling and plunging in her desire to get ahead, but I held her firmly, enjoying the sight of skewbald, bay, white and chestnut heads in perfect symmetry.

Evan had trouble holding Polar back too, and after a while yelled, "I want to go on another short gallop, OK?"

"You bet!" With the slightest touch my pony sailed into her beautiful, sweeping stride, this time leaving Polar behind.

I could hear the big horse's pounding hooves as Evan tried to bring him alongside, but there was no catching Scarlet as she flew over the yielding prairie trail.

As we neared the blackened tree that had been struck by lightning, I turned a laughing face and said, "Beat ya!"

"I'd like to say we weren't trying but it wouldn't be true," he grinned ruefully. "I just hope we're better at jumping than you two or Polar will start sulking!"

I was pretty eager to see the white horse perform, seeing how I'd volunteered to help try turning him into a competition squad horse, so I sat up and watched with great interest. As soon as he left Scarlet's side Polar seemed less confident and pranced nervously as Evan lined him up to approach a solid looking bank. I was glad to see Evan sat lightly in the saddle and that his hands were quiet, keeping a steady, light contact, but thought his lower leg could be a little more positive. He could have timed the take-off better, but the horse made a reasonably good shape through the air before landing neatly to pick up and canter on to the ditch. This he cleared easily, mainly, I felt, because there was an improvement in the rhythm and impulsion but I didn't like the nervous way Polar was holding himself.

"What do you think, Dana?" Evan turned to look at me and I was touched by the anxious expression on his good-looking face.

"Pretty good," I said reassuringly. "You've both got talent."

"Phew!" he pretended to wipe sweat from his brow. "You'll take us on for training, then?"

"Of course she will," Lucy was grinning. "Go on, Dana – show Evan and Page how it should be done!"

"Don't make it sound like I'm some kind of show-off," I objected. "Anyway, your turn to jump, Page."

"Not on your life," she backed off hurriedly. "That bank's too high for Petal and me, but we'll do the ditch if you like."

"There's another one just behind it," I pointed. "Do both and make it a double with a bounce between them."

"*You* can do that. We'll just keep it simple," Lucy trotted Petal forward.

They were going so slowly that the skewbald pony barely cleared the first ditch, with an ungainly action halfway between a slow hop and a slither. Page, trying not to laugh, followed and made a far better job of it on the chunky, short-legged Blade, but she didn't attempt the second one either.

"It's down to you, I'm afraid, Dana," Evan smiled at me. "As Lucy said, show us how it's done, and make this our first lesson."

"OK," I said reluctantly, still not wanting to seem like a

41

conceited know-it-all. "Technically you seem fine but your horse seems to lack confidence, so that's what we've got to work on. Watch Scarlet. She'll show you what you're aiming for."

My own, supremely confident mare, approached the bank at a smooth canter, perfectly balanced with hocks actively engaged. She judged the take-off exactly, lowering her head, lengthening her neck and preparing to spring. Rebalancing herself by shortening her neck and raising her head, she folded back her forelegs and propelled herself upward. The moments of suspension, landing and recovery were textbook perfect and our getaway stride took us the short distance to the first ditch, again taken with a silky precision followed by a classic bounce stride to clear the second. Scarlet was enjoying herself so much that I wheeled her in a shallow curve and took the three jumps again, this time in reverse order. Evan's face was an absolute picture when we came to a halt after clearing the bank the second time.

"I'm wasting my time here, Dana! You make Polar and me look like a pair of complete novices. We'll never make that squad!"

"Sure you will," I liked the way he was looking at me again. "A little practice, that's all you need. Come on, these jumps are wide enough to go over side by side as a pair. Let's see what Polar thinks of that."

As soon as the white horse was cantering alongside us I could see the difference in his whole attitude. His outline and impulsion improved, his tail stopped its nervous swishing and his dark eyes were bright as he looked ahead at the bank. This time he took all three, including the bounce stride approaching the smaller ditch, with an aplomb that had definitely been missing on his first attempt.

"That was fabulous!" I was genuinely thrilled with them both. "You see, you *can* do it."

"He felt very different that time," Evan's eyes were shining. "He usually messes around up here, seems a bit unsure of the wide open space, and you saw what he was like in the woods, kind of nervous and easily distracted."

"What's he like in the show jumping ring?" I asked. "Maybe he'd be happier in a more confined space."

"He can freak out more or less anywhere," Evan was being very frank. "And as you say, he's got the talent, so it's pretty frustrating."

"We'll work on it," I promised, turning back to the other two. "Do you want to jump again, Lucy? You and Page could try the pairs approach."

"Are you crazy? You can all keep going if you want, but Petal and I are happy to start walking home."

"It's OK, I'll come with you," Page brought Blade in beside her.

"We may as well go too," Evan said. "That last round is a good note to end on; I've never seen Polar so happy."

"Great," I smiled at the excitement in his voice as we turned the horses to follow the sedately walking Petal.

"Does Lucy always ride this slowly?" Evan muttered. "You two must spend your trail rides out several miles apart."

"Not really. Scarlet and I just put in extra lengths, cantering circles and weaving in and out of trees and stuff. It's good practice for Pony Club games."

We all seemed to be getting along very well, chatting

43

easily as the horses enjoyed the cooling-down walk on long reins, and it already felt as though we'd known each other for ages. The prairie spread before us with all its wild, rugged charm and even I had my bearings now because we were approaching the dark, humped shape of the hill I'd seen from Cornell Hall's garden. I stared at it with interest, and then caught my breath as a figure moved into focus on its summit. He had his back to us, focusing his attention on the land ahead. Surely, I thought, he's looking toward the house – and the sun flashed briefly as he held field glasses up to his eyes.

"He's spying!!" I said in surprise. "That man over there is spying on your uncle's house, Lucy!"

Chapter FOUR

Instead of the indignant outburst I expected, there was no response from my friend, and when I·turned my head I saw she'd slithered to the ground and was holding Petal's off-fore hoof and gazing anxiously at it. Evan and Page, their backs toward me, were gathered around her with Page just about to dismount as well. She handed Blade's reins to Evan and bent to look at the skewbald pony's foot.

"What's the matter?" I quickly brought Scarlet to a halt.

"Petal's gone suddenly lame," Lucy said. "Page thinks she's picked up a stone."

"Yup," Page took a fearsome looking gadget from her pocket. "There it is, lodged right up against the frog. Very painful."

With one deft movement she flicked out the hoof pick part and gently removed a sharp pointed stone. Lucy led her pony forward at walk, then turned and trotted her back toward us so we'd get a clear view of her movement.

"Perfect," Evan said. "She's completely sound, so no damage done."

"That's a relief," Page snapped the multi-tool knife shut and swung back into Blade's saddle. "Hey, Dana, what were you saying about a spy just then?"

"There's someone looking at the house from up there," I pointed to the hill.

"No there isn't," Lucy screwed up her eyes against the sun. "You're imagining things again!"

"I am not!" I said indignantly. "He was there earlier too – I saw the light flashing on his binoculars."

"Well he's gone now," Evan said peaceably. "Probably

just a hiker using the vantage point of the hill to get his bearings."

"What – *twice*?" I was still irritated at Lucy's crack about my imagination.

"As Evan said, it's easy to get lost up here," Page joined in. "We sometimes meet little groups of hikers and have to give them directions."

"Yeah, maybe," I said grudgingly, scanning the distance for another sight of my *spy*. "Though I wouldn't have thought he'd need it since we're nearly back at Cornell Hall now."

"Oh that's right, I can see the trees surrounding it," Lucy stood up in her stirrups for a better view. "Do you and Evan want to come in, Page?"

"Uh – no thanks," she said hurriedly and I could see my friend was hurt.

"It's not you," Evan explained to her kindly. "It's – um – it's your uncle. He's well known for chasing anyone off who comes near the place."

"We brought our dog over here one day and he chased a rabbit through the fence," Page said. "Mr. Harmon told us he'd shoot Buster if it happened again."

"Oh, terrific!" poor Lucy groaned. "I'm really sorry."

"It's not your fault," Page said good-naturedly. "But it might be an idea to OK it with your uncle before you invite us over."

"We'll see you tomorrow anyway, won't we?" Evan looked anxiously at me and I felt that glorious bouncy sensation again. "You said you'd help with the training again."

"Definitely," I promised. "Can we start off in your schooling ring?"

"Ah," his face became shuttered. "It would probably be better if we meet up in that clearing in the woods, like today. You don't need to ride all the way along the road, just cut through the trees like we did earlier."

"OK." I personally thought the well-fenced ring we'd seen would be more suitable for the nervous Polar, but maybe there was a problem. "See you in the morning, then."

"That was weird," I said to Lucy as the two of us rode up the weed-strewn driveway to the house. "They've got that great ring, perfect for training, so I wonder why Evan didn't want to meet at his place?"

"Maybe he and his sister have a foul, bad tempered old relative who threatens people with guns like I have," Lucy said, clearly disgusted at her Uncle James's behavior.

"Calm down," I looked at her in surprise. "I've never seen you get so mad so often!"

"You'd better get used to it, because I'm not going to let my uncle get away with acting the way he does. We came here to help, so he can at least be civil. If I want our friends to join us they will!"

"There's probably no need for Page and Evan to come here," I tried to soothe her.

"That's not the point!" Her eyes were still blazing.

"Don't get upset, Lucy. You know you hate being involved in a fight."

"Not this time," she said, squaring her shoulders. "In fact, I'm looking for one as soon as I get in that house. Uncle James won't know what hit him!"

I was feeling a bit like that myself, but it was such a shock to see my gentle, timid friend like this. When we reached the horses' field she handed me Petal's reins and

47

said, "Do her for me will you, Dana? I want to get this out while my temper's up."

I watched, open-mouthed, as she strode off toward the house, her silky blonde hair swinging defiantly. Checking Petal's off-fore hoof carefully, I untacked and brushed her down and watched her trot happily across the grass as she followed the ever-exuberant Scarlet. I stayed at the gate for a while, making sure they both settled down, then carried the tack over to the shed where we stored it. I felt reluctant to go indoors and found myself wishing I could live out here with the horses for the rest of my stay. Cornell Hall was not the most welcoming place at the best of times, and the thought of discovering Lucy in floods of tears while her angry old uncle yelled at her was just too horrible. I stepped inside and listened, then padded quietly along the narrow front passage to the wider inner hall leading to the kitchen. Kay and Mervyn were in there, talking together as he sat in his wheelchair and she busied herself at the sink.

"Sorry," I don't know why they made me feel awkward but they did. "I was looking for Lucy."

"Thought she was still out riding with you," Mervyn's sharp eyes surveyed me. "Unless she's in the front of the house somewhere. I wouldn't know, not being able to get the chair around those corners."

There was a whine of self-pity in his voice and I had to force myself to smile sympathetically at him. "It must be awful for you and I – um – hope your legs will be better soon."

"Thank you, dear, but the doctors say it will be a while yet."

I couldn't think of anything else to say and while I did genuinely feel sorry for him I couldn't help being irritated by his unctuous manner. Muttering an excuse, I took off again, glancing inside the rooms I passed in the hope of finding my friend. There seemed to be no one around so I went upstairs to the bedroom we were sharing. That, too, was empty, but through the open window came the sound of voices so I rushed over and peered out. There, against the backdrop of trees that blocked our view of the paddock, were Lucy and her uncle, and although I couldn't make out their words it was clear from the body language that an argument was taking place.

Lucy, arms crossed and chin tilted defiantly, was the one doing all the talking, while Mr. Harmon, his brows lowered like hoods over his eyes, stared silently at her. I saw my friend give the familiar toss of her fair hair as she stopped laying down the law, and waited for a growling outburst in response. But still the old man said nothing, his arms hanging at his side and his face turned completely toward her as if he was scrutinizing each feature carefully. Lucy hesitated, and then bent forward slightly as if listening, before slowly turning away and walking back toward the house. I immediately rushed out of the room and halfway down the stairs so I could catch her.

"Lucy!" I hissed. "Up here!"

She was walking along the narrow hall, her expression puzzled, and she paused briefly before continuing toward me. I waited till we were both in our room.

"What did he say? Your uncle, I mean. I saw you talking to him out there."

"It took a while to find him," she sat down on her bed. "I knew I had to see him while I was still fired up, and when I finally tracked him down in the garden I thought we were in for a huge fight."

"You were brave to take him on," I said with feeling. "I think he's scary."

"I don't often get mad, but Uncle James has upset my Mom, my dad, probably my brother all those years ago, and now my friends. So for once I was angry enough to say something." Lucy shook her head. "But he didn't react the way I thought. At first he was kind of dismissive, as if he didn't care what I said, and that made me even madder. I gave him a real hard time about the way he's treating us and how I hated hearing he'd threatened the new friends we'd made. He suddenly went all quiet and just stood there looking at me while I ranted."

"I could see him from the window. He was watching you like a hawk, as if – as if he couldn't believe what he was seeing."

"That's exactly it! He told me he was completely amazed at how much I looked like Helena Harmon. He said it twice actually, and the second time he added, "I must show you the portrait of her as a young woman.""

"Who's Helena?"

"My grandmother – no, my dad's grandmother, so my great-grandmother."

"Your great – so that makes her Uncle James's mother?"

"Yes, he and my dad's dad were brothers."

"Gotcha," I said. "So, you look like one of your ancestors – no big deal, right?"

"You'd think. Uncle James was really weird about it, though. He said he'd seen the likeness right away, but when I got mad at him just now it was extraordinary. That's the word he used – extraordinary."

"It must be to have shut him up like that! Going by his

reputation he likes nothing better than a good fight, so it would have to be something special to distract him."

"It's kind of spooky," Lucy shivered. "Being told you look like a dead person."

"Your great grandmother was obviously blonde and beautiful when she was young, so what's your problem?" I teased her. "Go and find your dad and tell him. Maybe he can use the likeness to persuade your uncle to be more cooperative."

"I wish! Or maybe I don't, because if Dad can't talk the old goat into doing something about the repairs to the fence we'll probably leave this dump and go home soon."

"Aw, I don't want that to happen," I said immediately. "It would mean I couldn't help Evan get a place in the competition squad."

"And spend your time being bossy and leaping over impossible jumps," Lucy gave me a good-natured shove. "You're right, Dana, I enjoyed riding with Page today – we could have fun here if my uncle would be reasonable. I'll go and see what I can do."

She went off to talk to her family while I scribbled down some ideas for the next day's training session. I'd like to say that I leaped out of bed at the crack of dawn the following morning, eager to start work, but unfortunately early mornings and I don't seem to mix. In the winter when Scarlet is stabled at night I have to use *three* alarm clocks to make sure I get up in time to take care of her before I go to school, and even then my Mom sometimes has to shake me awake! The sun, though filtered by the overhanging trees, was fairly streaming through the bedroom window by the time I opened my eyes and Lucy's bed was not only empty but already neatly made. Groaning at myself, I staggered to the bathroom, and then looked blearily at the outside world through our open window. In my dopey, half-awake state I thought I had a case of déjà vu, feeling I'd definitely seen my friend and her uncle in exactly the same spot I was seeing them now.

Of course you have, you dumb cluck, I told myself, shaking my head to clear it. They're both standing more or less where they were yesterday, when Lucy was giving him her ear bashing.

This morning, though, the body language was quite different, with none of the aggression and conflict that had been so clearly defined. As I watched, Lucy actually laughed at something her uncle said and his craggy old face brightened and became instantly softer. I threw some clothes on, dragged a comb through my hair and ran downstairs, reaching the hall just as Lucy stepped inside the front door.

"Look at that," she called cheerily. "Sleeping Beauty's awake at last!"

"You should have called me," I said grouchily.

"I practically beat you over the head with a pillow and you just grunted and rolled over," she said, tossing her shiny, properly brushed curtain of hair. "Don't worry, I've checked on the horses and given them breakfast. Scarlet's fine and raring to be a teacher horse, she told me."

I gave a reluctant grin. "Thanks, Lucy. Sorry, I'm terrible at waking up. I should have warned you."

"It's OK – oh, guess what? Uncle James says we can all practice here if we want. There's a field around the back of the house we can use."

"Great," I said, heading for the kitchen. "You seem to be getting along really well."

53

"I don't know about that," she said cautiously. "He's still being difficult about getting the fence repaired, though Dad seems to think the old boy is coming around to the idea."

"Did you tell him off about Page and Evan's dog?" I put some bread in the toaster and poured cereal into a bowl.

"Uncle James says that was a mistake – he'd been plagued by a gang of local kids and thought our two were part of them. He doesn't even own a gun, so he didn't mean it anyway."

"You'll have to convince Page of that before she'll risk riding here," I laughed. "I'll just eat this and we'll go and meet them, OK?"

"OK," she helped herself to a piece of my toast. "I'll head over and start getting the horses ready, seeing as I left it all to you last night."

"You were on a mission," I winked at her. "And ranting at your dear Great Uncle seems to have worked wonders!"

After she'd gone I quickly finished my breakfast, then washed the dishes and stacked them to dry.

"I should think you would tidy up!" Mervyn moved silently in his well-oiled wheelchair. "It wouldn't be fair to my wife, having to clear up after such a late-comer."

"Sorry," I mumbled. "I overslept."

"No problem, as long as Mr. Harmon doesn't find out. Off you go, and have fun on your ponies."

"Yeah, we will." I forced myself to smile at him, feeling guilty that I found him so completely irritating. "Uh – thanks, see you later."

I hurried along the hall and back upstairs, where I collected my notes and riding hat, and set off for the paddock. Scarlet, already brushed and gleaming, was at the gate while Lucy finished tidying Petal. Once saddled and bridled, both horses seemed as eager as we were to join our new friends, and we set off through the woods at a brisk warming up pace. Evan, with his sister, was already in the clearing and looked up eagerly as we arrived.

"Hi," Evan rode his stunning white horse toward me. "I thought maybe you'd changed your mind about getting involved with this."

"Not us," I was really starting to enjoy the happy feeling I got every time he looked at me. "We're still up for it, and I've got some ideas for you."

"Great," his blue eyes were warm but I could see a faint crease of worry on his forehead. "You're going to build a really big course for us to tackle, I guess."

"Not at all," I'd given it a lot of thought. "The first thing to do is get you and Polar relaxed and enjoying yourselves. You both seem a little wound up about jumping, so we're going to have a Pony Club Games morning instead."

"Yeah?" he looked surprised. "How's that going to improve our chances of getting picked for the squad?"

"Well, for starters it'll do wonders for your fitness with all the speed work it involves. It also sharpens reflexes and builds up a great rapport between you and your horse. We'll need Page and Blade to get involved too, if that's all right."

Evan looked across the clearing where his sister was talking to Lucy. We could hear them laughing and it was obvious they were getting along really well.

"Page will be fine with that as long as Lucy's involved too. They kind of have the same attitude about competition."

"Mm," I was glad Lucy had made a new friend and tried hard not to feel a bit left out. "We'll get started then, OK?"

We began with an impromptu version of a flag race, using some broken branches stuck in Evan's marker cones, making it a flat out relay. The four horses thoroughly enjoyed thundering up and down the course, and although Polar shied nervously the first time Evan leaned over to reach his *flag*, he quickly got the idea and joined in with great enthusiasm. It was a beautiful morning, and although we laughed and clowned around a lot, I kept the momentum going so that everyone got a thorough workout.

"Phew!" Evan panted as sweat rolled down his face. "You're wearing me out, Dana, but isn't Polar doing great?"

It was true, the big white horse was showing none of the signs of anxiety he'd displayed the day before and was revealing a marked competitive streak as he strove to get over the finishing line ahead of the other ponies.

"He's doing *too* great as far as Petal and I are concerned," Lucy said. She had dismounted and was lying flat on her back while her placid pony nibbled at the grass beside her. "We need a break, Dana."

Scarlet and I were hardly out of breath, but as Page and Blade were also showing signs of wilting I thought maybe she was right.

"We can go to our house," Evan offered. "The horses can have a drink and a rest while we do the same."

The white-fronted house was very pretty and, as I'd noticed before, its gardens and paddocks were immaculately kept. We got a warm welcome from Evan and Page's Mom who settled us comfortably under a big umbrella on the terrace where we could keep an eye on the horses while we enjoyed the cold drinks she and Evan carried out to us. Page and Lucy, still acting like they'd known each other forever, stayed talking and giggling in the shade while Evan led me across to a vantage point so he could show me the layout of the grounds.

"There's the winter paddock," he pointed. "And over there is the one currently being used by Polar and Blade."

"I noticed the field next to the trail we used has been plowed," I looked across to where the land sloped gently toward the road.

"Yeah, Dad's going to reseed to get some good spring grass for the boys."

"Good idea," I shielded my eyes against the sun. "And down there, next to the road is your schooling ring. We spotted it when we drove past on our way to Cornell Hall."

"Yeah," his face took on the wary, shuttered look I'd seen before. "We – uh – chose that spot because it's the flattest area of ground we've got. Everything else is on a slope."

"Yeah, I can see that, but the ring looks terrific," I said. I was worried by his odd attitude but I've always felt it's better to take the direct approach. "So, can we use it for the jumping practice you and Polar are going to need?"

"No, sorry." Without looking at me Evan turned away. "It's not an option, I'm afraid."

Before I could even open my mouth to ask why, he walked quickly away, leaving me snubbed, bewildered and alone.

Chapter FIVE

After the initial shock wore off I convinced myself I'd simply gone about asking in the wrong way and that Evan would apologize for getting in a huff and explain the problem. But he did neither, remaining detached and silent the whole time we were getting our horses ready for the next part of the training session. When we got back to the clearing he was no better, merely nodding briefly when I asked him to do anything and staying as far away from me as he could. Because Polar had enjoyed the fun of mounted games so much, I decided to continue the competition theme with a short course of low jumps to be taken in relay style as a team.

This time, though, I could see from the start that the idea was not going to be a success. Even though the fences were well within Polar's scope he seemed unhappy, and made lots of mistakes, rushing some fences and flattening badly over others. When, after a couple of messy attempts, he refused point-blank to go around again I called a halt. I could see quite clearly that the problem emanated from Evan, who was tense and uptight, causing the white horse to react with the worst display of nerves I'd seen.

"Try to relax, Evan," I smiled at him, hoping to recapture the close familiarity we'd shared earlier.

His only response was to shrug and say, "I thought I was."

There was a defensive, surly note in his voice and I found myself suddenly out of patience with him.

"It doesn't look that way to me," I slid to the ground and started dismantling the makeshift jumps. "If you're not going to try there's no point carrying on with the training."

"But you said you'd help," he said, meeting my eyes for the first time.

"It's a two-way process," I retorted, looking directly at him. "I can't do anything if you don't cooperate."

"Sorry, Dana," he jumped off Polar's back and came toward me. "I didn't mean to spoil things; I just got a little uptight."

"Well, that's the first thing you've got to learn to control." I knew I was doing what Lucy called my *bossy teacher* act, but felt strongly that he really needed it. "Your horse is very sensitive and picks up immediately on your negative mood."

"You're right, he does," he sounded surprised, as though he hadn't made the connection before. "OK, I promise I'll stop being a grouch, so don't give up on us, please."

He really was incredibly appealing when he looked at me like that, and I felt the familiar churning in my insides.

"I think Polar's too upset to do any more jumping. He'll end up dumping you again if we push him now. We'll just take them all for a gentle trail ride through the woods. If he relaxes enough you can jump a log or two, but only if it will leave him with a good memory of the process."

"You're really clever," he said humbly. "I'm sorry I'm so useless."

"You're not," I said shortly.

I was itching to ask him outright what the problem was. We'd been doing fine before I asked if we could use the ring, and I wanted to know what had made things change so abruptly. I opened my mouth to confront him but then shut it again. Evan, though obviously anxious to have me around, still showed no sign of coming up with a voluntary explanation so I decided to keep quiet until he did. After all, I figured, I was supposed to be helping with his riding, not solving his personal problems.

The ride through the pretty, shady woodland was very pleasant and Evan seemed to make a great effort to be attentive and friendly but he still didn't mention the reason for his earlier bad temper. Scarlet and I enjoyed ourselves in our usual manner, cantering across grassy clearings and through shallow water and jumping enthusiastically over fallen trees and the banks and ditches around the meandering stream. After a while Evan followed us through a natural jumping lane of logs and shrubs, ending with a hefty bank into a wide stretch of water. He'd now recovered his buoyant mood, which meant that Polar was again relaxed and happy, and put in a superb athletic leap to clear the bank.

"If you two jumped like that all the time, you'd have no trouble getting picked for the squad," I remarked.

His blue eyes were rueful. "But then you wouldn't be helping us."

There was no mistaking the warmth in his voice and I hoped I wasn't blushing.

"Mm," I said, as coolly as I could. "You didn't seem to feel that way earlier."

He hesitated, but just as I thought he was about to explain, Lucy and Page came splashing along the stream toward us.

"We saw you jump that massive bank," Lucy laughed. "And thought there's no way we're going over that so we came the wet way with a nice paddle."

I glanced briefly at Evan and saw the moment was lost.

"Polar jumped it well," he said, in a joking voice, "and our teacher was pleased with us."

"I've never seen you work so hard to be the teacher's pet," Page grinned in her laid back way. "Evan's not the best student, but I guess you've already found that out, haven't you, Dana?"

I smiled back without making any comment. We finished the ride with some fun, playing a noisy, childish and highly entertaining game of *cops 'n robbers*, with Evan and me as cops giving the *baddies* a head start in their getaway run. We spent half an hour or so chasing between, over and across the trees, glades and stream in the woods, whooping and yelling as we tracked the robbers down. Evan thoroughly enjoyed himself and it was amazing to see the difference in Polar, who, untroubled by any signs of rider tension, thundered joyfully around, taking all kinds of obstacles in his stride.

"There they are!" I pointed ahead where two fat equine rumps were disappearing into another clump of trees. "Go get 'em, Evan – oh and jump that big fallen tree on the way."

The white horse cleared the hefty tree trunk in perfect athletic style and I thought that was a good point at which to call a halt. As Evan herded the two giggling robbers back toward me I marveled at the change in both horse and rider now that they were both relaxed and happy.

"Give your boy the afternoon off. He deserves it," I said. As I spoke I liked the way Evan leaned forward and gave Polar lots of praise. "Scarlet needs a rest too, so I'll go and turn her out as well."

"She looks as though she could still do an entire cross-country course," Lucy said, out of breath. "Neither of you has even broken into a sweat, and we're all completely wasted!"

"We've got a long way to go before we're as fit as Dana and

Scarlet," Evan said, giving me his knee-buckling grin. "Come back to my house instead, and we can all chill out there."

"No thanks!" The thought of going to his house when he hadn't apologized or explained his strange behavior made me feel angry again. "Maybe some other time."

"Oh," he said, looking crestfallen. "See you tomorrow, then?"

"Maybe." I was upset and didn't feel like making things easy for him. "Give me a call later."

Before he could say any more I turned Scarlet and started heading toward Cornell Hall. Or at least I thought I did.

"Dana!" Lucy yelled from behind me. "Where are you going? It's this way."

"You're no help, Scarlet," I muttered to my pony as I turned her around again. "You've got no more sense of direction than I have!"

"So," Lucy waited for me to join her. "What's with you? I got the distinct impression you liked Evan, so why the cool treatment just now?"

I shrugged. "If he wants someone to sweet talk him out of his bad tempers he's picked the wrong girl."

"Oh, right. I noticed he got all moody when we left their house. What was that all about?"

I shrugged again. "Same thing as before. I suggested using their ring for training and he got all weird again."

Lucy took her feet out of her stirrups and dangled her feet below Petal's stomach. "He's probably got his reasons. Could be family problems like me."

"Yeah, I realize that, but if so he should tell me and not cut me dead and act like a big moody kid," I said bitterly. "I'm doing my best to help him here."

"Do you want me to ask Page what it's all about? She

and Evan are pretty close, she's bound to know what the problem is."

"No thanks. Evan should be upfront and tell me himself."

"You've got him all worried now, thinking you won't go and see him again," Lucy said as she eyed me speculatively. "And it's not just because of the riding training – I think he really likes you."

"Whatever." I thought I made a good job of sounding not bothered but I don't think I fooled her.

To our surprise there was someone in the paddock when we got back. Uncle James, busy with pitchfork and wheelbarrow, was clearly waiting for our return.

"Good ride?" His eyebrows were still lowered but he sounded much more friendly.

"Terrific," Lucy dismounted quickly. "You don't have to clean up the field, Uncle James. We do it every evening."

"Oh I can see that, yes," he patted Petal gingerly. "You do a very good job, looking after your pets."

Pets! You'd think Scarlet and Petal were a couple of goldfish.

"No, I – um – I was just hanging around here so I thought I'd make myself useful," he went on.

"Thank you," Lucy sounded quite touched, and for a moment I thought she was going to reach up and kiss his cheek.

Her uncle's expression made it clear that he'd like that, and for the first time I felt a pang of sympathy for the difficult old man. He waited patiently while we rubbed the ponies down and watched with us until they'd settled to their grazing.

"You know the picture I mentioned earlier, Lucy?" he said diffidently.

"The portrait of Helena Harmon?"

"My mother, yes," he cleared his throat noisily. "I'd like you to see it."

"Now?" She was very tired after what had been, for her, an energetic morning, but his face was so hopeful that she smiled sweetly. "Sure, OK, Uncle."

I wouldn't have minded a look myself, but I knew when to be tactful.

"I'll go and see if I can help with lunch," I walked with them back to the house and then I turned left toward the kitchen while Lucy and her uncle continued along the hall.

Once again Mervyn and Kay were there, with Kay busy at the stove while her husband watched from his wheelchair.

"Hi," I smiled politely at them. "Can I give you a hand with anything?"

"You can set the table," he said at once. "I was just about to start but you'll be quicker on those strong young legs."

"OK," I said amiably, washing my hands at the sink. "Just tell me where everything is."

While I gathered up silverware and placemats he hovered irritatingly beside me.

"My wife tells me," there was that annoying whine in his voice again, "that she saw Mr. Harmon pushing a wheelbarrow out in the field earlier. I hope you girls aren't making extra work for him."

"No we're not," I said shortly. "He said he just did a little cleaning up while he waited for us."

"He was waiting for you?" Mervyn looked almost shocked. "Why, may I ask?"

It was sheer irritation that made me shrug and say, "I don't know."

"Well, where is he now?"

I shrugged again and he sighed impatiently.

"Kay, go and see if they're still in the field, would you?"

"The lunch will spoil if I do," she replied in her colorless, flat voice.

I finished laying the table and said brightly, "There you go. I'll go and find everyone."

I shot through the narrow doorway, glad he couldn't follow, and walked along the hall in the direction Lucy had gone. At the far end was a heavy looking door and I hovered outside it, not wanting to interrupt but hoping for an invitation inside. Just as I was about to tap on the paneled wood the door opened and Lucy, looking distinctly shell-shocked, came out.

"Hi," I said eagerly. "So – is she like you? Your great-grandmother, I mean."

"Oh," she stepped back, holding the door open. "Here's her portrait. What do *you* think?"

It was a big, formal oil painting of a young woman in an old fashioned evening gown. Diamonds sparkled in her ears and at her throat and her blonde hair was swept up into an elegant chignon, but the face that looked out at me was unquestionably Lucy's.

"Wow!" I walked a little closer. "It's exactly like you, Luce – just slightly older and more elegant."

My friend giggled, almost hysterically. "Good old Dana, that's a perfect description really, isn't it, Uncle James?"

The old man had been fiddling around at the drawer of a desk but he gave a brief smile as he walked toward us.

"I'm glad you both like it. Did Kay send you to call us to lunch, Dana?"

"Oh yeah," I took another peek at the portrait as he ushered us out of the room.

"Do you think Kay will mind if I just take a sandwich outside?" Lucy watched her uncle double lock the hefty door. "I've – I've got a lot to think about and I'd like to be on my own for a while."

She saw the hurt glance I gave her and added hurriedly, "Except for Dana. You'll come and have a picnic with me, won't you?"

"Sure," I considered it a much nicer idea than eating in a kitchen with creepy Mervyn. "I'll go and ask if it's OK."

"Of course," the old man had a nice voice when he wasn't roaring. "I, too, prefer to lunch alone so Kay will be happy to accommodate you, I'm sure."

The housekeeper had made another batch of her wonderful soup but poured some into a flask for us without comment when I asked. I made a quick sandwich to go with it and was out of the room before Mervyn, who'd gone looking for Mr. Harmon, according to his wife, came back.

"Where shall we go?" Lucy said, looking a bit pale, I thought. "To the horses' field?"

"No, I think Mervyn might have gone there looking for your uncle. Let's have a high rise picnic in that old tree we found."

Lucy had enough trouble climbing with two hands, so apart from cramming a sandwich in her pocket, couldn't help much, but I climbed up and down a couple of times and we were soon enjoying our food on one of the broad, central branches.

"There's chocolate mousse for dessert, only slightly squished," I said, grinning at my friend. "Are you OK?"

"Sure," she slurped her mug of soup inelegantly. "Just a little flustered, that's all."

"About seeing the portrait?" I nodded understandingly. "It must be weird seeing someone who looks that much like you."

"It's not just that," she hesitated. "Did you notice Helena – my great-grandmother's jewelry?"

"Something nice and sparkly. I think there were earrings, didn't notice any bracelets, but definitely a necklace; that really stood out."

"It did, didn't it?" She took a deep breath. "The necklace, made of high quality diamonds and a single sapphire, is the reason my dad and my uncle haven't spoken for fifteen years."

"Get out!" I gaped at her. "How come?"

"I haven't gotten my head around it yet. Apparently Helena bequeathed her necklace to the next female Harmon. She had two sons, remember, my Uncle James and my grandfather. Uncle James never married and Granddad Harmon only had one son."

"And that's your dad, Joe Harmon," I said, showing I was listening intelligently.

"That's right. Dad married my Mom and because she was now Molly Harmon, Dad thought she was entitled to the necklace but Uncle James got mad and said no."

"Why? Oh, I get it. To be a proper Harmon descendent you've got to be *born* into the family and not marry into it – it's funny, really, because Helena herself only became a Harmon through marriage."

"You're very quick," Lucy said. She put down her soup on the broad branch and patted my head admiringly. "Uncle James seemed to think my dad was trying to, in his words, *pull a fast one*, which means get hold of the necklace by cheating."

"Right," I was following the plot so far, "So is that what caused the falling out?"

"No, Dad said he understood Uncle James's objection and they stayed in touch, and even brought Ty here to see him when he was tiny."

"Ah, but then you were born," I waved my sandwich around. "And this time your dad said you had a genuine claim to the necklace."

"You're really good at this. I had to get Uncle James to go through it twice, it sounded so complicated."

"It's completely straightforward. Helena, your great-grandmother, willed the necklace to the next-born female Harmon – that's you. So why aren't you wearing it with your jeans and T-shirt? Because for some reason your Uncle James wouldn't agree and he kept the necklace for himself and *that's* what caused the quarrel."

"That's it exactly. How could you *know*?"

"Your dad's a sweetheart." I really like Joe. "He wouldn't have fought with a cranky old man unless it was something major, and his little baby being swindled out of a valuable heirloom is pretty huge, you have to admit."

"But Uncle James doesn't think he's doing any swindling. He says he's only looking after it till I'm twenty-one, which is what Helena wanted."

"That sounds reasonable," I said, surprised. "So why won't Joe go along with that?"

"Because my uncle is so stubborn and unreasonable that he didn't explain it properly, that's why! I think he was very hurt when dad cut off all contact, but he's too proud

69

to admit it and he was too proud to make the first move to make things right. Now he's suspicious of dad's motives in coming back, but – but he's really taken to me, mainly because I look so much like Helena."

"And he likes you," I nodded. "He did right from the start, and when you stood up to him he liked you even more."

"Yeah, maybe," she said as finished her soup. "He's a weird old thing, but I've kind of taken a liking to him too."

"And you're happy to have him keep the necklace for another six years?"

"Absolutely. Helena was twenty-one when she married and the portrait was painted soon after. I could get all glammed up, wearing the necklace with my hair piled up like hers and have a studio photo done when I'm the same age."

"Your uncle will love that," I smiled at her. "So have you seen it? The real thing, I mean?"

"Yeah," her eyes shone. "That's why the study is locked at all times – it's in there. Uncle James showed me."

"No wonder you looked shell-shocked," I laughed. "I thought it was from seeing the portrait, but you'd just been shown your very own priceless jewelry. Your dad is going to be so thrilled."

"Oh no," she groaned. "This is the worst part. My uncle doesn't want me to tell my parents yet. He wants to see if they'll carry through their offer of help even without the prospect of getting the necklace."

"He's a scheming old devil." I had a sneaking admiration for the tricky old man. "Are you going to tell them anyway?"

"No," she said slowly. "Probably not. I want my uncle

to see that my dad's an honest person, not someone who's helping out just to get his hands on the diamonds."

"Duh!" I teased her. "You're as devious as that old man is! You're a proper Harmon in every way!"

She pretended to smack me and I quickly shinned onto a higher branch to get out of her way.

"Hey!" I was now looking out across the prairie and I could not believe my eyes. "Mr. Spy Man is there again! Honestly Lucy, you've got to see this; he's up on that hill and his binoculars are definitely trained on Cornell Hall!"

Chapter SIX

Below me Lucy stood up cautiously. "I can't get up there, you know I can't."

"Sure you can," I leaned down, grabbed her hand and hauled while she scrambled up, trying to get a foothold. "Put your other hand on the trunk there and pull yourself up."

"I can't, I'll fall," she wailed and I gritted my teeth, bracing myself against the branch as I tried to hoist her up to join me.

Eventually, after a lot of girly squealing, she reached the higher branch and stood clutching the tree trunk fearfully with her eyes screwed shut.

"Lucy!" I shook her and she squeaked again.

"Don't, Dana, you'll make me fall."

"You're perfectly safe and you're up here to look at the spy, remember!" I was out of patience with her. "So it might be better to open your eyes and use them!"

With her arms wrapped around the tree she peered nervously in the direction I was pointing.

"Nothing!" she said bitterly. "After your bossing me around to get up here there's no one there. Honestly, Dana, you put me through all that for no reason!"

I whipped around and stared. The hill, dark and humpbacked, seemed to glower at me without a trace of someone on its summit.

"You missed him," I balanced right on the edge of the branch to get a better view. "He *was* there; I could see the sun glinting on his binoculars and everything."

"Yeah, well," she said as she closed her eyes again. "I still think you imagined it, and now I've got to get down from here."

"It's easy," Even though I felt guilty she was scared I was annoyed she didn't believe me. "Don't be such a wuss."

It took another ten minutes before she'd even try climbing down to the big, comfortable branch where we'd picnicked, and by then I'd scraped my arm and banged my knee twice trying to help her move.

"It's no good getting mad at me," she opened one eye. "I can't help it, I'm really scared."

I rubbed my battered knee and looked at her. She was very pale and the hands that still clutched the oak were trembling slightly.

"Oh Lucy, I'm sorry," I felt a rush of compassion. "I shouldn't have made you climb up here. Do you want me to go and fetch your dad or a ladder or something?"

"No, just stop swarming around like a monkey, and hold on to me again."

By the time we reached the ground we were both dripping with sweat and covered in dirt, leaves and bits of bark. Lucy shook herself violently, spat out a twig, and looked at me.

"Best fun I've ever had. We must do it again sometime!"

I pulled some leaves out of her hair and burst out laughing and soon we were both rolling around in fits of giggles.

"And after all that," I touched my sore knee gingerly. "You still didn't get a look at Mr. Spy Man!"

"I refuse to believe in him," she said, throwing a handful of grass at me. "It's probably an optical illusion, making you think one of those weird stunted trees is a person."

"What about the binoculars, then?"

"The sun shining on an old bottle or something," she

said, looking down at her filthy T-shirt. "I'm past caring anyway. I need a shower and some clean clothes."

"Me too," I stopped doing my *I am right* act because she wasn't giving me a hard time about scaring her. "And me first!"

I sprinted (slightly painfully!) toward the house with Lucy belting after me, yelling all the rude names she could think of.

"Now girls, girls," Mervyn steered his wheelchair across our path as we hurtled across the drive. "Please be quiet. We don't want to upset Mr. Harmon, do we?"

"Dana and I don't," Lucy obviously found him as irritating as I did. "But I don't think he'd mind us making a little noise. My uncle says he likes having some life around the place."

"Is that what he said?" Mervyn looked quite taken aback. "It's not the impression I got, I must say."

"OK, we'll keep it down," I said peaceably. "Won't we, Luce?"

My friend's response was to grin wickedly and dart past me, reaching the front door before I realized what she was up to. I pounded along the hall and up the stairs in an effort to catch her but she'd already slammed the bathroom door shut and I could hear her laughing as she turned on the shower. Once we were both clean and dry she was very concerned by the long, angry looking scrape running down my arm and insisted on putting antiseptic cream on it.

"I don't know how you can climb around in trees the way you do when you know you can get hurt," she said, shaking back her freshly washed curtain of hair. "You're just not scared of anything, are you, Dana?"

"Not really," I agreed. "Like in riding, I can never

74

understand why anyone's too scared to tackle a tricky cross country course or a hefty parallel in show jumping."

"You're lucky. A lot of people find stuff like that totally scary – me more than most," she said as she smoothed the last of the cream gently into my skin.

"Yeah, I guess so. We'll find something quiet and peaceful to do this afternoon, then. That way you won't be terrified and your uncle won't come gunning for us because of the noise."

"What do you suggest?" she grinned at me. "A little knitting? Some stamp collecting, maybe?"

"Lucy," Joe's voice sounded from downstairs. "Are you up there?"

"Yeah, Dad," she flung the door open.

"We're going into town to get something. Do you and Dana want to come?"

I nodded and gave her the thumbs up.

"OK, we'll be right down," she checked her reflection in the mirror. "I look good enough for the city streets, don't I?"

"Far too gorgeous for the town of Cornell – they won't know what hit them!" I spiked my hair up a bit more. "Let's go."

To our surprise Joe and Molly were hitching the pony trailer to their car.

"What –?" Lucy stopped when she saw them.

"It's not for the horses," Molly explained. "It's for fence posts."

"No! You mean Uncle James has agreed to put in the new boundary?"

Her dad winked at her. "Hop in the car and we'll tell you on the way."

75

"So," Lucy sat forward on the back seat as Joe drove carefully through the rusty old gateway. "How did you talk the old man into the new fence?"

"It wasn't me – I thought *you* must have said something," Joe looked at her in the rear view mirror. "I saw you go into his study and was expecting you to tell me about it at lunch time only to find you'd gone off on a picnic."

"We went to the horses' paddock thinking you'd be there, and saw Uncle James on our way." Molly said happily. "He was practically civil to us both for once and said he could see our point about the boundary fence."

"I thought he was actually going to say *call a builder in, spare no expense*," Joe joked. "But he's still being very cagey and said he was only prepared to pay for the materials."

Lucy nudged me hard. "How did you react to that?"

"I told him we'd be happy to do the work – and well, he just grunted."

"But it was a nice grunt," Molly beamed at us. "And there was no sign of that horrible grouchy glare he usually gives us."

"Great," Lucy said lightly. "Looks as if you're starting to convince him you're genuine."

"As I said, I thought *that* was your doing. What did Uncle James want you for anyway? Earlier, I mean, when he showed you into his study?"

"Oh, he wanted me to see Helena's portrait," Lucy said quickly. "He showed Dana, too."

I nodded innocently, hoping I wouldn't give the necklace secret away by saying the wrong thing.

"Really?" Molly turned around to look at us. "Helena

was Joe's grandmother; I guess Lucy told you that, Dana. I remember seeing the painting briefly when we came here with Ty. She was very young and elegant in it, I recall."

"And the spitting image of Lucy," I said. "It's the first thing that strikes you."

"Well, Lucy wasn't even born when I saw it, but Joe remarked on the likeness many times while she was growing up," Molly looked regretful. "It makes me sad to think there's such a strong family resemblance and yet Lucy's been denied her birthright –"

"Molly, we agreed not to say anything about this till Lucy was older," Joe broke in and Lucy nudged me again.

"I'll be black and blue if you keep doing that," I hissed.

"I just wanted to make sure you didn't blurt out we know about the you-know-what."

"The necklace?"

"Shh!" She jabbed me again.

"Hey, they're not even listening, and now I've got sore ribs as well as a bad arm and bruised kneecap!"

Lucy looked at the front seat where her mom and dad were deeply engrossed in their own whispered conversation. "Sorry, Dana. Oh look, we're here!"

We'd pulled up outside a big DIY store on the edge of the town.

"We're probably going to be a while," Joe told us. "There's a lot to load on the trailer and I want to price some other stuff as well."

"Will you two be OK on your own?" Molly asked. "I mean, I could come to the shopping mall with you. It's only across the way, but you'd rather have a look around without me, wouldn't you?"

"Yeah, we would," Lucy said honestly. "So what should we do – meet you back here in an hour?"

"That's fine," Joe was peering at the list he'd brought with him. "You've got your cell phone if there's any problem, right?"

"Yup," we jumped out of the car and walked along the path linking the store to Cornell's shopping mall.

It wasn't exactly big city chic but there were nice clothing stores and a really trendy shoe place. I was eyeing some outrageous wedges in the window when my phone rang.

"Hi – Dana?" It was Evan's voice so I deliberately kept any enthusiasm out of my own.

"Hiya."

"Um, we, Page and I that is, wondered if you wanted to come over? Unless you're too busy or something."

"We're out," I said tersely.

"Oh? Oh, right." He sounded so disappointed I relented a little.

"We're in Cornell, in the shopping mall for an hour or so."

"We've got our bikes, so we can be there in ten minutes and meet you," he said eagerly. "Is that all right?"

"Sure." Even without seeing his face I was feeling happy. "See you soon."

I flipped my phone shut and grinned at Lucy. "They're biking over to see us. He seemed pretty eager."

"Poor old Evan's devastated you've gone all cold on him," Lucy went to nudge me again, and then remembered my aching ribs. "Be nice to him, you cruel creature!"

"I'm still waiting for an explanation about the ring," I reminded her. "I hate it when people go all secretive on me, and I seem to be surrounded by all these mysteries today."

"Evan will tell you his in his own time," Lucy said. "He likes you. But promise you won't say anything about Helena's necklace to anyone, please? I don't want my dad finding out I know."

"I promise." Privately, I was pleased it was only me she wanted to share her secret with; it showed that despite the connection she and Page had made, Lucy still considered *me* her best friend. "But I hope your uncle hurries up and realizes your parents are good and honest."

"So do I, but he'll probably wait to see that they put the work in on his fence," Lucy said ruefully. "He's a wicked old devil!"

"But you like him," I laughed and gave the funky shoes one last look. "Shall we go into that shop over there? They've got some great posters in the window."

We were browsing happily when a raucous group of young guys came crashing along the mall, playing loud music and yelling stupid remarks to each other.

Lucy, timid as ever, held my arm and said, "Don't go out till they've gone. They look like trouble."

I wasn't that bothered, but obligingly hung back, watching the gang make their disruptive way through the mall. They were nearing a sort of crossroads where four entrances merged into the shopping center and I suddenly caught sight of Evan and Page approaching along one of the aisles. They must have been able to hear the racket kicked up by the gang because I saw Evan reach out and grab his sister's arm, drawing her back, much as Lucy had done to me. Once the four guys had sauntered past I saw Evan's blonde head peek out as he checked their progress. He then stepped forward, followed by Page, and they walked rapidly into the mall.

"Oh look, there's Page!" Lucy peered out of the window. "That gang is gone so let's go and meet her."

I followed her out of the shop wondering why the incident I'd seen had made me feel slightly uneasy. Evan's pleasure at seeing me soon drove the thought out of my head and we had a good time hanging out in the cool, comfortable surroundings of the mall. Evan bought me a can of soda and took me over to a gift store where they had a nice display of carved horses. We spent some time admiring them, then left the shop and strolled back toward Lucy and Page who were sitting on a bench, heads together, giggling as usual. This time I didn't hear the gang's approach. They'd switched their music off and were padding silently behind us.

"Look at this guy!" the tallest, about the same age as us and only slightly shorter than Evan, pushed past and blocked our way. "Very nice, Evan. She looks *too* nice for a Momma's boy like you, though."

Evan, his face suddenly pale, muttered, "Shut up Nick, what's it to you?"

The dark haired Nick stretched out a hand to touch my face and I sidestepped quickly.

"Get lost, creep!"

"What did you call me?" he said, putting on this tough, swaggering act.

"You heard me," I said and, to his obvious surprise, I took a step toward him. "Or are you deaf as well as stupid?"

I felt, positively felt, a shudder go through Evan as he took my hand and pulled me away.

"Let's go, Dana, they're not worth bothering with."

"Yeah, *Dana*, go, and run away like your sissy new boyfriend," Nick, his face twisted and ugly, started to come after us but one of his pals said urgently, "Security's coming, Nick. They said they'd kick us out if there was any trouble."

"Trouble? Not from me," said Nick, and before he turned away he jabbed a finger viciously in our direction. "Not this time anyway. See you, Dana and Momma's Boy."

"You all right?" Page and Lucy had only just spotted the confrontation and were running toward us.

"Yeah," Evan wouldn't look at me. "They're just mouthing off, it's no big deal."

"They need to be taught some manners," I said, fuming. "Bunch of low life bullies."

"Oh cool it, Dana, don't start," Lucy was looking nervous. "Come on, we've got to go back now."

Evan and Page walked with us to the DIY store, shaking hands politely when they met Joe and Molly.

"They seem nice," Molly said approvingly as we drove away. "If Uncle James agrees, you'll have to invite them over."

"He's fine with it, and said we can use the top field for riding training, but we've got jumps and stuff all set up in the woods behind Evan and Page's house."

"Oh right, though I'd have thought you'd use that good looking schooling ring of theirs," said Joe. He didn't notice the grimace I made. "Still, the fact that your uncle's happy to have your friends at Cornell Hall is another breakthrough, like the new fence."

"Things are definitely looking up," Molly agreed.

I stayed quiet, the feeling of unease so strong within me that I couldn't share their optimism.

As soon as we got back I helped unload the trailer and

then took off for the paddock. Scarlet and Petal were grazing together in the far corner, but when I started walking across the field my pony lifted her head and whinnied a greeting.

"Come on, Scarlet," I called, standing still with my arms outstretched. "Come and see me."

She moved forward at once, flowing into the beautiful, free canter she performed so well.

"I thought we could share an apple and chat," I leaned against her, breathing in her sweet meadow grass smell. She took the pieces of apple gently, flicking her intelligent ears as I told her all my woes.

"So, do you think I'm being stupid?" I stroked her velvet nose. "Worrying about Evan like this? See, I'm pretty sure Polar's problems all stem from his rider. When Evan is confident and happy his horse is fabulous and when he's not poor old Polar is just a bag of nerves."

Scarlet pushed her head against me.

"Ow," I said. "Watch the sore arm. Oh, and the ribs and knee! See, Scarlet, the trouble is I can't do anything to help Evan until he helps himself. If he's going to act jumpy and back off anything that scares him he and Polar are never going to make that squad. And they're not going to have much fun either!"

My pony blew loudly down her nose as if in agreement.

"I know," I pretended to understand what she'd said. "Some people are naturally more nervous than others, like our lovely Lucy, but if it's making life difficult for your horse then you've got to *do* something. Petal's OK. She's so placid nothing upsets her, but Polar's a complete mess when Evan gets nervous."

"You've got that right," Lucy had come up quietly behind me. "Page told me why her brother won't use the ring."

83

"Because he's scared?" I turned to face her.

"Not of the jumps – he truly, genuinely wants to be good enough to compete. No, it's that gang we met in town – Nasty Nick and his pals."

"Yeah?" I had recognized Evan's fear of the gang.

"Yeah. Nick's just a bully and he likes to pick on Evan. They all used to walk along the main road by the schooling ring when he was practicing and climb on the fence, jeering and name-calling. Evan got more and more wound up, and that's when Polar started refusing fences and ducking out. They had a crashing fall one day and since then Evan's refused to ride down there. Instead he hides out in the woods where Nick and his gang can't see him."

"He should stand up to them," I said furiously. "If he doesn't he'll always be scared and Polar will always pick up on it."

"That's easy for you to say – you're not scared of anything," Lucy said. "Evan obviously isn't made like that – so what are you going to do – refuse to help him anymore – even stop seeing him altogether?"

Chapter SEVEN

I pretended to think about it. "No," I said slowly. "I'll keep trying as long as he does too."

"Hah!" Lucy could see right through me. "You want to keep on seeing him because you think he's cute."

"Possibly," I tried to be all dignified. "I really do like him but I'm getting a little frustrated with his riding because I know he isn't giving it a hundred percent."

"As long as you're not going to dump him altogether," Lucy couldn't really care less about the training. "Because if you did Page wouldn't talk to me. She's completely loyal."

"You've always got me!" Again, I felt quite hurt. "Or am I still too much of a know-it-all and not enough fun?"

"I never said that!" she pretended to take a swipe at me. "You're the best, but you have to admit it's great with the four of us; there's more going on."

"Listen to you!" It was my turn to make fun of her. "As if you haven't got enough going on in your life, what with inheriting fabulous jewels and becoming your uncle's favorite and keeping deep, dark secrets from your mom and dad!"

"I am *not*," she said, turning pink. "I explained about not telling them –"

"Yeah I know, I'm only joking," I put my arms around Scarlet's neck and gave her a hug. "And don't worry, I'm backing you up and I promise I won't let it slip to Molly and Joe."

"Thanks, Dana." My friend watched indulgently as I gave Scarlet one last kiss. "I guess we should offer to help them with the fence project. It's going to be a big job for just the two of them."

"Great. I always like to spend a vacation dragging fence posts around," I grumbled as we walked back to the gate. "Especially when we know your crazy old uncle could afford to pay someone to do it."

"He's gotten into the habit of not spending any money," Lucy was quick to defend him. "Just like he's developed this grumpy, people-hating character over the years. I think the real Uncle James is a kind person; he's just gotten used to hiding it because he doesn't have any real contact with anyone and he's lonely."

"Huh? You've sure changed your opinion of him since we arrived," I said, looking at her as we clambered over the gate. "You couldn't wait to leave the old goat and get back home as fast as possible. It's not just that we're having a good time, is it – you really are starting to get fond of your grouchy old uncle, aren't you?"

"Yeah, we've sort of clicked," Lucy admitted. "And I really, *really* want him to like my dad too."

"He will," I said confidently. "Joe's totally honest and the old man is already starting to realize it. Once Uncle James sees your mom and dad put all the work into that new fence everything will be fine and you'll become a real, close-knit family. I just know it."

Unfortunately the close-knit family thing wasn't much in evidence when we tracked Joe, Molly and the old man down.

"I've told you, you're not bringing mechanical diggers and workmen onto my land," Uncle James's heavy eyebrows were drawn together in a scowl. "You two seem to think I'm made of money."

"No we don't," Joe spoke quietly but I could tell he was running out of patience. "We just want a good, professional job done so your boundary fence will stay in place for a long time to come."

"Mervyn's done the repairs for years," the old man barked. "And saved me a fortune doing so."

"I have to disagree with that," Joe was becoming more heated. "Mervyn's botched attempts are what caused the fence to keep breaking down, and the end result of that is the major falling out between you and your farmer neighbor."

"George Barlow? Pah!" Uncle James made a gesture of disgust. "Just because his animals strayed a couple of times he demanded we go halves on a professionally built fence, that's what caused the fight. He's another one who seems to think I'm a millionaire!"

"It was a very generous offer of Mr. Barlow's to share the cost, and you'd have been wise to take him up on it," Molly said sharply. "Just as you'd do well to listen to your nephew now."

"Hah! I knew you didn't mean it when you offered to do the work for me," the old man turned his beetle-browed gaze suddenly on Lucy. "You told me your parents were good people, but here they go letting me down again."

"They're doing nothing of the sort," Lucy responded with spirit. "If you'd listen instead of shouting you'd know that."

"It's all right, Lucy, I don't want you involved," Joe put his arm around her. "I'm quite prepared to dig every hole myself. I just wanted a decent job done for your uncle's sake."

"There you are, you see, Uncle!" Lucy took a step forward.

Uncle James looked at her flashing blue eyes and up-tilted chin and gave a reluctant smile. "Yes, Lucy, I see. All right you two, you can bring in a digger and its driver, but I'm not paying for a bunch of builders' laborers."

"Molly and I are the laborers," Joe took her hand. "We might take longer, but with proper foundations we'll give you a fence that'll last for years *and* placate Farmer Barlow."

You've probably noticed that, as in most communications with Uncle James, I kept quiet through the whole argument. This isn't like me. I've usually got plenty to say, but a) I thought it was all Harmon family business and b) the old man still frightened the life out of me. Again, this isn't something that happens a lot. I tend not to be afraid of anyone, but I found the bad tempered Uncle James distinctly scary and admired the way my normally timid friend, Lucy, stood up to him. Which is what I told her when we were riding our ponies through the woods the next morning.

"You think I'm brave?" she said and grinned at me. "That's a first. Come to think of it, it's the first time I've heard *you* admit to being scared. I can't understand how you can take on anything from big fences to bullies yet be intimidated by a dear old man."

"Dear old man!" I scoffed. "He's terrifying! I've never seen anyone look literally red with rage like he did when he thought your parents were trying to get out of repairing his moldy old fence. There were practically sparks coming out of his eyes!"

"Nonsense," Lucy said briskly. "Uncle James just gets a little overheated and needs to be straightened out occasionally. He's no trouble at all."

"Not for you, maybe," I was still going to treat the old fellow with extreme caution. "So, what about today? Will you and Page join in if I set up a cross country course?"

"Do we have to?" She is *so* lazy. "I was exhausted after playing that cops 'n robbers thing. I want the chance to talk anyway, so can't we just have a normal trail ride instead?"

"That's not going to progress Evan's competition training, is it?" I said severely.

"But it would be a good warm up," Lucy tried to persuade me. "You said Polar needs a lot of confidence building."

"That's true," I thought for a minute. "Maybe we could go across the prairie again; sort out whatever it is that makes him spook up there. Only I think I know already."

"Yeah? You think it all stems from Evan, don't you? Maybe Nick and his gang hang around on the prairie and that's what's freaking him out."

"I bet not," I said. I couldn't imagine the bully gang trekking up to the remote and barren prairie in the hope of finding a victim. "Still, there's only one way to find out."

Evan was so delighted that I'd turned up again that he was ready to agree to anything I suggested.

"Sure, we can ride on the prairie," he said at once. "Only I thought you were going to concentrate on our jumping."

"Technically there's not much wrong with what you're doing," I said. "When you're both relaxed you're terrific, so – um – I thought a nice leisurely trail ride to unwind would be a good way to start today's session."

I saw Lucy hide a grin as we all turned our horses and started back through the wood.

"I want to show Lucy our spy anyway," I told Evan as we rode side by side. "That guy I saw on the hill has been watching Cornell Hall again. He's always doing it, but my friend doesn't believe me."

"I'll make sure I keep an eye out for him," Evan

promised, but when we reached the sandy trail of the prairie land there was no sign of anyone else. The bleak, tawny colored landscape stretched before us, empty and almost silent.

"Not even a bird singing to keep us company today," Lucy remarked. "Let alone Dana's imaginary spy."

"I did *not* imagine —" I began hotly but Page the peacemaker broke in quickly. "We're bound to see him eventually. Let's try Jagged Tor first."

Once I was cantering, feeling the power and speed as Scarlet skimmed across the short, yielding turf, I forgot everything else and just reveled in the fantastic sensation it always gave me. We pulled up beside the huge rock and gazed around us.

"The prairie isn't like anywhere I've seen before," Lucy said. She and Petal were already slightly out of breath. "It looks like – like a huge blanket that some giant tossed in the air and spread all over the ground."

Her description, though fanciful, was pretty apt. The terrain, mostly in a patchwork of brown broken only by the odd splash of color, was strangely bleak and featureless, lacking the verdant green of trees and grass marked by fences, gates and the well used trails we were used to riding at home.

"There *are* landmarks around," Evan pointed out a few rocky outcrops and an occasional lone, twisted tree.

"It's pretty harsh up here in the winter," Page explained. "So the trees get stunted by high winds and the sandy soil means nothing much grows except coarse grass and the odd patch of heather and gorse plants."

"The yellowy green stretches are boggy marsh, aren't

they?" Lucy gave a little shiver. "I wouldn't like getting stuck in one of those."

"You said there's a trail going through there though, didn't you?" I was intrigued by the *no-go area*. "Can you show us where it is?"

I could see by Evan's face he wasn't eager.

"We could ride past when we're on our way home, I guess," he said, looking uneasy at the idea. "But I don't want to take Polar along the trail – he hates it."

Mm, I thought. 'Your horse only hates it because he picks up negative vibes from you!'

We carried on riding across the *safe* part of the prairie and I made sure Polar jumped the bank and ditches we'd done before. Today, armed with the confidence built from our successful tandem exercise, Evan had the white horse clearing the jumps perfectly, and I marveled at the difference in them both. All four of us played another silly game of chase and again Polar thoroughly enjoyed himself.

"He feels fitter already," Evan gave his fabulous grin. "Hardly blowing and still raring to go."

The gently undulating land had sloped uphill to another vantage point and I suddenly caught sight of something moving away in the distance.

"Look at that," I pointed. "Is it another horse?"

Evan screwed his eyes up against the sun. "Where?"

"Over there in the marshy part," I stood up in my stirrups. "It can't be a hiker. He's going too fast. I bet it's our Spy Man!"

"No way," Evan was positive. "I told you, no one with any sense would take a horse through there. Are you sure it's a person?"

"You're as bad as Lucy. She thinks I'm imagining things," I said, now quite annoyed. "Let's get closer and you'll see."

"OK," he sighed and headed Polar in the direction of the marsh.

"Where are you going?" Page, still some way behind with Lucy, called out.

"Dana wants to check out the marshes."

"Oh count me out!" Lucy shrieked at once. "I don't want to get sucked in by any boggy ooze."

"We're not going *in*," I said impatiently waiting for her to catch up. "Just to the edge."

"Well I don't want to go anywhere near it!" she said, stubbornly refusing to follow.

"You two go that way while Lucy and I go along the main trail, and we'll meet up outside Cornell Hall's grounds," Page suggested. "You're a lot faster than we are so we'll probably take about the same time."

Evan and I cantered at first, the ground beneath us soft, dry and perfectly safe, but as we got nearer and nearer the swathe of yellowish green he slowed the pace to trot, and then walk. He was silent, too, and the easy, happy closeness we'd been sharing was replaced with an awkward air of restraint. I noticed too that Polar's demeanor had changed, the free-striding action gone and the highly-strung, tail swishing nerves becoming more apparent with every step.

"Hey, relax you two!" I tried joking. "We're just taking a look, it's no big deal."

Evan made a visible effort to keep cool. "Sorry. Polar hates the marsh, so I get a bit uptight."

"I think it's the other way around," I said gently. "You're wound up and that's what's making your horse nervous."

"You really think that?" Evan turned his head jerkily to look at me and as he did so a bird suddenly flew out of a patch of scrubby gorse to our right.

Polar, already twitchy, reacted by shying violently, almost throwing his rider from the saddle. Evan lost a stirrup and his grip on the reins, but managed somehow to stay aboard as his horse broke into a panicky gallop. I went after them, feeling a sickening jolt as Scarlet's hind leg slipped from the trail, dropping her hoof momentarily into the soft, sinking mud of the marsh. My brave pony barely seemed to register the problem, maintaining her speed and momentum to stay close behind the bolting Polar. I kept talking, speaking in calm, soothing tones and soon Evan was able to bring his horse's pace down with a series of half-halts. Soon the white horse was standing quietly on the narrow, twisting trail, his sides heaving.

"All right, Dana." Evan's voice was bitter. "You've seen the marshes we told you about. Maybe now you understand why we don't ride this way."

"Yeah, all right," I looked down at the black, boggy slime clinging to Scarlet's off hind leg and bit my tongue so I wouldn't point out it wasn't *my* fault we were in the wretched swamp. "Are you OK?"

"Just about," he started turning Polar carefully. "And you'll notice there's no sign of anyone else around."

I ignored the sarcastic edge to his voice and looked around. The marsh surrounded us, looking deceptively innocent, the only sign of the danger within showing in the sickly hue of vegetation covering the treacherous mud beneath it. Evan was right, there was no one else in sight and I was miserable that not only had I upset the ultra

94

sensitive Evan again, but also the incident had undone a lot of the good our previously relaxed ride had done for Polar.

"I'm really sorry Polar got spooked," I said, after we'd ridden carefully and in a definitely huffy silence back to the safety of firm, sandy soil. "But it honestly wasn't my fault."

I saw the tense, hunched line of Evan's shoulders soften as he tried to relax.

"Yeah, I know. Sorry, Dana, I shouldn't take it out on you when my crappy riding lets me down."

"There's nothing wrong with your riding, I keep trying to tell you that. It's just an – an attitude problem."

"You think? So you're saying if I get that straightened out everything else will fall into place?"

"More or less," I tried a smile and was relieved when his mouth curved in response. "You've got a great horse there, but he picks up every emotion so you have to stay positive for him."

"Right," he sank his chin to his chest. "I'll work on it."

I could tell now wasn't the time to keep nagging him, so I changed the subject completely and by the time we met Lucy and Page we were back on good terms, laughing and talking together.

"You've made your beautiful pony dirty," Lucy's eagle eyes had spotted Scarlet's muddy hoof.

"She dipped her foot in the marsh just to prove we've been there," I said facetiously. "No sweat, don't worry."

"I'm worrying about something more terrifying than a boggy marsh," Page said solemnly. "Lucy wants us to go in for a snack."

"Into Cornell Hall?" Evan was incredulous. "What

about your uncle? He's not known for being exactly welcoming, Lucy."

"*He's* all right," Lucy said airily. "Come on, you wimps, Kay was baking this morning and she's a fantastic cook. Couldn't you just murder a slice of home made cake right now?"

"Don't say murder!" Page pretended to faint, but started to follow unwillingly as Lucy started riding along the neglected, weedy drive.

Evan and I rode side by side again, but despite his stream of lighthearted banter, I knew he was feeling as reluctant as his sister about the visit. Despite Lucy's assurances about her uncle I started to feel a little nervous myself, peering around to see if he was about to challenge us with one of his bad tempered tirades.

"We'll ride the horses around the back to the kitchen door," a totally cheerful Lucy called back to us. "I'm sure Kay will bring a drink and some cake outside for us all."

"Oh, no she won't!" Mervyn's wheelchair rattled clumsily across the gravel toward us. "My wife knows better than to encourage troublemakers like these two. Mr. Harmon's made it perfectly clear he doesn't want riffraff anywhere near his house, so I suggest you turn right around and get yourselves off his land!"

Chapter EIGHT

Lucy, the new feisty Lucy, reacted immediately.

"My *friends*," she emphasized the word strongly, "are staying, Mervyn, and I suggest you check with your *employer*," she emphasized that one too, "and get your facts straight before – before –"

"Shooting your mouth off?" I suggested helpfully.

From his wheelchair Mervyn glared balefully up at us both. "You're not trying to tell me your uncle agreed to let these two in? I recognize that white horse; I've chased it off myself before."

"Well, you got it wrong then and you've got it wrong now," Lucy swept past him on Petal. "Come on, guys."

The three of us followed a bit uncertainly, making sure our horses gave Mervyn a wide berth. When we reached the back door Lucy hopped off her pony and handed me her reins.

"Don't let her eat any of the cabbages or anything. I'm going to get our cake," she squared her shoulders and marched into the kitchen.

"So," Evan cleared his throat. "Do we dismount or what?"

"I'm staying put," Page said darkly. "In case we get chased off again."

I slid to the ground and stood between Petal and Scarlet. "You heard Lucy. We're staying whether we like it or not."

My friend reappeared very quickly, triumphantly carrying a tray loaded with cold drinks and half a chocolate cake.

"Here you go," she glanced up at the other two, still firmly in their saddles. "What are you doing? Sit down over there and don't let your horses –"

"Eat the cabbages, yeah," Evan and Page dismounted reluctantly and we led the ponies to an ancient table and bench.

The cake, I have to admit, was absolutely delicious and at the first bite we all cheered up a lot.

"Kay was all right with you, then?" I asked with my mouth full.

"Perfectly," Lucy said firmly. "Not that she ever says much."

"I thought Mervyn would have warned her not to feed the local thugs," I grinned at Evan when I said it.

"He hasn't been in. He's probably hunting Uncle James down to tell him all about it," Lucy finished her cake and wiped her mouth appreciatively. "I bet my uncle's put up with Mervyn all these years just because of his wife's cooking."

"He's the handyman you said, didn't you?" Page was licking crumbs off her plate. "It's a little weird having a disabled handyman, isn't it?"

"It's called loyalty," Lucy told her severely. "At least I suppose that's what it is."

I thought it was very pleasant enjoying the summer sun and admiring Kay's neat rows of vegetables in the patch of kitchen garden she'd made from the surrounding jungle, but Evan and Page couldn't seem to settle.

"That was great, really great," Evan stacked plates and glasses on the tray. "But we should be going. I want to – um – practice some jumping before Polar has his midday rest."

"And you also want to get out of here before Mervyn sets my uncle on you," Lucy glared at him. "Don't be such cowards, you two!"

Evan flushed and fell silent and Page said quickly, "It's not cowardice; it's called wanting a peaceful life."

"That's right," Evan shot her a grateful glance. "We used to get yelled at by Mervyn or Mr. Harmon if we just rode a little too close, so we've gotten into the habit of avoiding them both."

"And I'm not eager to meet up with your uncle, seeing as the last time I saw him he threatened to shoot our dog," Page reminded her.

"Uncle James doesn't even have a gun," Lucy was exasperated. "So he didn't mean it, and anyway he thought you were someone else."

"Yes I did, and I apologize," Uncle James had arrived, pushing the wheelchair. "There's nothing to worry about, Mervyn. These aren't the ones who did the damage last year."

"Even so, I don't think they should be here," Mervyn spun the chair abruptly away from the old man's hands and moved toward the back door.

I think we all expected Uncle James to react, but apart from a noticeable tightening of his jaw he said nothing, turning back to look at us instead.

"I – ah – I see you've been enjoying some of Kay's excellent cake," his face cracked into what I recognized as a smile. "Good, good."

He was trying as hard as he knew how to welcome his great-niece's friends, and I could see Lucy was touchingly proud of him. Mervyn, without another word, slunk off and we spent quite a while talking to the old man until Scarlet got bored and started fidgeting and nudging me.

"Why's he doing that?" Uncle James patted her uncertainly.

99

"She's a girl and she wants to get back to work," I said and he smiled indulgently.

"A ball of fire, just like all you girls! Off you go then, but – um – Evan and Page, you can stop by any time."

"My friends will never believe that invitation," Page clowned around, pretending to faint along Blade's neck as we rode back down the drive. "They've all been chased away from Cornell Hall's boundary about a million times!"

"Maybe your friends were among the bunch who used to steal the apples and stuff like that," Lucy was immediately on the defensive. "You can't blame my uncle for defending his property."

"We don't, we're just surprised that he seems like a pretty nice old guy," Evan said. "I didn't like that creep of a handyman, though."

"Yeah we're with you on that," I said with feeling. "Come on, we'd better get these horses warmed up again if you want to do some jumping."

Lucy and Page, predictably, didn't want to do any training, but they helped drag branches around to make different obstacles for our course. Because I was worried that Polar's confidence had been shaken by his scare on the marsh earlier I did another fun session, starting off jumping as a pair, then getting Evan to follow closely as Scarlet and I did the route, and finally watching the two of them as they tackled it alone. Evan had recovered his good temper and rode extremely positively, resulting in a perfect clear round done with great style and panache.

At the end of the session we put all four horses in Evan's top paddock to give them a couple of hours break. It was fascinating to watch them. As soon as we let them loose the sensible, single-minded Petal shook herself vigorously from head to tail then took three steps forward, dropped her nose and started grazing. Blade rolled briefly in his favorite dust spot and followed her. They touched noses affectionately, his big bay head nudging her neat white and tan one, and then, staying very close, both happily began cropping the short sweet grass. In complete contrast, Scarlet, who always finds a new situation very stimulating, cantered twice around the field, stopping suddenly before whirling around and sailing back in the opposite direction. Polar watched her at first, his handsome head tilted to one side as if in surprise. When he decided to join her she skittishly took off again, giving her trademark high kicks as she went. They thundered around together for several minutes, in a symphony of movement and grace until Scarlet got bored. She then rolled thoroughly, over to the right, then the left, then right again while Polar stood looking at her with an expression I swear was indulgent pride. Just to affirm it was *his* field she was in, the big white horse lay down in the exact spot she'd used and waved his hooves skywards.

"He's trying to demonstrate his dominance," Evan was laughing with me. "Even though all he does is follow every single thing she does."

"Maybe his time to be leader will come," I said. "With all this new-found confidence he might surprise us all one day!"

Both horses did eventually settle down to some peaceful grazing while we lolled around in the shade, listening to music and generally chilling. We were having such a good time and getting along so well that I didn't want to spoil things by bringing up the sensitive issue of the ring. The shamefaced way Evan had reacted when Lucy half-jokingly

101

called him a coward told me he was very aware of the
problem he had with confrontation. I'm all for an easy life
but, as Lucy had recently found in the troubled relationship
within her family, there are times when the only way to
deal with a problem is to – well, *deal* with it. If Evan
stood up to the bullying tactics of Nick and his crew he'd
feel a whole lot better about himself, I was sure, and that
self confidence would be communicated to Polar who'd
respond in an equally positive way. Don't get me wrong, I
wasn't trying to interfere in Evan's personal life, but I knew
it was affecting the riding I was here to help.

"You're miles away," Evan poked me gently. "I've been
talking to you and you didn't hear a word."

"Sorry," I smiled at him, feeling a familiar tingle.

I didn't want that tingle to go away, so when he
suggested we get the horses ready for more cross-country
practice I found myself agreeing, even though I knew it
was show jumping in the schooling ring he needed. We
spent the afternoon riding the course we'd made in the
woods, which ended in the clearing where I'd first seen
him fall off Polar. He'd made huge improvements already,
and I could see he was working hard at keeping his attitude
positive and his approach fearless. Polar was cooperating
by responding enthusiastically, thoroughly enjoying his
jumping and showing no sign of ducking out or refusing.

Everything was going great, with the two of us
thoroughly enjoying making a competition out of the
session, riding the woodland course as if a fabulous
trophy was at stake. Evan had just taken Polar across the
stream and was turning him, curving in an arc to tackle
the next jump – a sizeable log landing in a wide, shallow

pool – when sheer chaos broke loose. We'd both been concentrating so hard we hadn't heard a stealthy rustling getting nearer and nearer. I did turn my head at the sharp cracking sound of a twig breaking but shrugged it off, thinking it was Lucy and Page returning from their more sedate ride. When the shrubs and undergrowth to Evan's right suddenly erupted in a tumult of harsh noise, and the tall, dark figure of Nick sprang forward, his features contorted as he yelled obscenities, I was so shocked that I stopped riding for an instant and Scarlet threw up her head and shied sideways. I recovered immediately, bringing her back onto the bit, slowing the pace and calming her quietly.

Poor Evan, ahead of me and right in the firing line of Nick's jeering, raucous presence, had no such luck and was thrown over his horse's head as Polar went into total panic mode. I heard the splash as he hit the water, and the cruel burst of laughter from Nick and the guy accompanying him, but had no choice other than to take off after the bolting white horse as he galloped, stirrups bumping and reins flapping, away from the terrifying noise.

I was sure he would head for home but, scared, he'd keep up the panic stricken pace and run until he hit the road. I stayed in pursuit, finally catching him as he thundered toward his paddock gate. There was a trickle of blood on his near fore leg and I quickly slid to the ground and checked him over. The cut was superficial but needed to be cleaned. I called out, hoping someone in the house would hear me, and Page and Lucy came running.

"Oh no, Evan hasn't fallen off again, has he? He's been so much better since you started helping," Page led the sweating Polar into the field and stroked him gently.

"Nick and one of the others are up there in the woods," I said tensely. "They jumped out at Evan, so he didn't stand a chance."

"Is he all right?" Lucy's eyes were wide.

"Don't know, and I'd better go back. Will you take care of Polar – he's got at least one cut."

I turned Scarlet, who as usual was taking all the excitement in stride, and cantered back into the woods. There was no sign of Nick, which was probably just as well because the way I was feeling I'd have happily run him down. About half way in I met Evan, soaked to the skin and limping slightly.

"Are you OK?" I slithered out of my saddle and ran to him.

"I'm all right." The sullen, withdrawn note was in his voice. "What about Polar?"

"Page is checking him over, but I think it's just a few scratches."

Evan ran a hand through the thick blonde hair now plastered wetly to his forehead and said briefly, "Good."

"Did – did you – um – speak to Nick?" I knew it was a stupid question as soon as I asked it.

He shrugged, not meeting my eyes, "What's the point?"

"The point is," I felt a surge of anger. "He's got to stop this."

"What do you suggest? That I take him *and* his gang on? Don't think I'd get very far."

"Nick's the ringleader, so just deal with him," I said. I couldn't believe he was being so negative.

He shrugged again. "If I don't give him the satisfaction of reacting he'll get bored soon."

"Yeah, right. He's already stopped you using your own

schooling ring and now I suppose you're going to stop riding in these woods, are you?"

"Maybe, for a while. Like I said, he'll get bored of coming out here and forget it. He used to cause trouble up at Cornell Hall but he doesn't bother any more."

"Yeah, because he got completely chased off!" I was furious that he was refusing to face the truth. "And that's what you should be doing."

His only response was to lower the hooded lids even further over his eyes and trudge away, leaving me speechless and once again alone.

CHAPTER NINE

"Come on, Scarlet," I said, feeling that only my pony was in tune with me. "There's no point in hanging around here."

I rode her back through the woods and, given the fighting mad mood I was now in, it was just as well I didn't meet Nick. Our carefully constructed *course* was all around me, the logs and branches we'd dragged around to make jumps across the stream, and in the clearing, the more elaborate fences made of hurdles, brushwood and poles all stood silently waiting. Although my main emotion was anger, I felt depressed and sad because of Evan's attitude, and for once had no inclination to put Scarlet over any of the jumps, so simply plodded dejectedly toward Cornell Hall. As my pony and I quietly approached the thick belt of trees around the grounds, I caught my breath in surprise. There, inside the perimeter fence, was Mr. Spy Man, binoculars in hand as he peered around. Just as I was about to shout, he gave a start and clamored rapidly back over the fence to scuttle immediately away in the direction of the prairie. I squeezed Scarlet's sides and put her into canter but as we started thundering after him, Uncle James's head appeared at the fence.

"Hey!" he called to me. "Is something wrong? Where's Lucy?"

"Back at Evan and Page's house," I said, inwardly cursing as I pulled Scarlet up. "Did you see that man running away just then?"

"Man? What man? I was just checking this part of my fencing when I heard you coming at me like a freight train."

"I saw this man," I explained impatiently. "He was on

your grounds and I think he must have heard you coming because he ran back and vaulted over the fence, just about where you're standing."

"Oh?" his hairy brows drew together in the familiar frown. "Not one of those hooligans we caught stealing the fruit off my trees?"

"He was old, well, middle-aged and I've seen him before, spying on Cornell Hall from that hill up on the prairie."

"He won't see much from there," the old man said. "Young Joe is right; it's all gotten a bit overgrown, too many trees crowding around."

"Well maybe that's why the spy man came in for a closer look."

"What's he looking for, then? There's nothing to see here, but I'll give him what-for if he trespasses on my land again."

And if you'd let me catch him you could have done that today, I thought, but merely said, "I'll just ride up to the prairie and see if he's still around."

"Right you are. Lucy's coming home soon, I hope?" his grumpy old face lit up just at the thought. "I wondered if she'd give me her thoughts about some other improvements around the place."

"Yeah, I think she'll be back shortly," I smiled at him and moved Scarlet away.

We cantered along the sandy trail with me having a good look around for the man I'd just seen running away from the Hall.

"If he's walking he can't be too far ahead," I told Scarlet and let her plunge into an exuberant gallop as we crested the slope.

The prairie stretched before us, wrapped in its tawny

cloak, timeless, mysterious – and empty. There was no sign of Mr. Spy Man anywhere so I assumed he must have doubled back somehow, probably to a spot further along the road where he'd parked a car. In the gloomy mood I was in I very nearly took off across the deserted expanse, feeling I could quite happily leave Evan's attitude way behind me. Poised on the crest of the dark humpbacked hill, I looked around me and decided it wouldn't be a good thing to do. It felt quite different up here without the company of my friends, and I could see how easy it would be to get lost, or worse still, make a wrong turn and find myself in the middle of the treacherous boggy marsh. Instead, I turned my pony and rode her back toward Cornell Hall at a sensible cooling down walk, and was lying in the paddock watching her crop busily at the grass by the time Lucy and Petal appeared. Scarlet raised her head and whinnied a greeting to her friend and I sat up and waved to mine.

"You all right?" Lucy took Petal's saddle and bridle off and released her immediately. "She doesn't need rubbing down or anything. We did her at Evan's place. So, why didn't you come back there with him?"

"Who?" I said, as if I didn't know. "Evan, you mean? Not a lot of point, I felt, seeing as he wasn't talking to me again."

"Yes he *was*," she said as she walked over and flopped down beside me. "If he was being stand-offish it's because he was embarrassed and ashamed about what happened."

"Falling off his horse?" I enquired facetiously. "That's no big deal."

"Oh, don't try to be funny. You're so serious about this stuff, you never *do* jokes! Look, Dana, Evan's really, *truly*, upset that he didn't stand up to Nick, but you seem to have even more of a problem about it. I suppose you want him to be a real macho hard man?"

"Of course I don't," I snapped. "But there's a big difference between that and letting yourself be walked all over by a loser like Nick. I'm supposed to be helping turn Evan into a competition rider, but every time he refuses to stand up to his fears it affects his riding and, more importantly, his horse, so it's a waste of time me trying."

"So you're going to walk out on him?" Before we came here Lucy would just have gone along with everything I said, but not any more. "And you call yourself a competitor? In my book giving up makes *you* a bigger coward than Evan, and I'm ashamed of you!"

I was so flabbergasted I could only watch open-mouthed as she flounced crossly away. As she neared the gate Uncle James appeared, and after a few words she went off with him without so much as a backward glance.

"Did you hear that, Scarlet?" I practically squeaked. "The nerve! Like any of this is my fault!"

Both ponies very sensibly ignored me and kept on grazing, so I lay back again, staring up at the lofty brilliance of the sky and feeling hurt and verbally abused. I stayed like that for quite a while, feeling very sorry for myself and misunderstood by *everybody*.

Eventually even Scarlet got fed up with me and took herself off to the far side of the paddock. I sat up, glared at her retreating rump, and then hauled myself to my feet and walked back to the gate. I could hear the noise of the mechanical digger Joe and Molly had brought in, and wandered toward the sound, knowing I'd always get a welcoming smile from those two. As I approached I could see Lucy and her Uncle James were there too, laughing at something Joe had said, and I stood back, sulkily reluctant to join them. They looked like a happy group with Uncle James's face stretched in his rusty, not-much-used smile as he fondly watched Lucy clown around with her mom and dad. It was a shame to think the old man had missed fifteen years of family togetherness because he'd been too stubborn to make the first move and explain about Helena's necklace. It struck me that my own attitude of bossy superiority, coupled with Evan's inability to communicate, could easily result in a similar rift.

You're an idiot, I told myself. 'Do you really want to leave here and never see Evan again?'

It wasn't a difficult one to answer. I liked Evan and wanted to keep on not only seeing him, but also helping with his ambition of becoming a competition squad rider. Being the impulsive, instant action type, as soon as I had it sorted in my head I pulled out my cell phone to call Evan, stepping back into the shade of the trees so I could see to dial. From here I had a clear view, not only of the Harmon family group and the big digger but also, hidden away behind overgrown shrubbery, Mervyn. His wheelchair was quite close to me in fact, but he was oblivious to my presence, so fierce was his concentration as he watched Lucy, Uncle James, Molly and Joe. The expression on his face was hard to read; an odd mixture of resentment and what looked like despair, and I wondered about it before shrugging and getting on with my call. Evan sounded utterly amazed to hear my voice.

"You all right?" I made myself appear very upbeat. "Dried off and everything?"

"Oh yeah. My leg hurts a little where I bashed my knee on a stone, but Polar's is fine and he isn't lame."

"Great. I – um – thought maybe you'd come over here for tomorrow's training, then. We can build some jumps in that field Lucy's uncle said we could use."

"Yeah?" he still didn't quite believe it. "I mean, if you'd rather, we can use the woods again."

I realized it must have taken quite an effort to say that and made my reply deliberately casual. "Nah. It'll do Polar good to try somewhere new."

"OK, great, thanks, Dana and – um – thanks for not making a big deal out of – you know."

"No problem," I said airily. "See you in the morning."

As I walked forward I glanced over to the spot where Mervyn had been covertly watching and saw he was now gone. I waved cheerfully at the Harmon family as I came up to join them.

"Another one come to inspect our handiwork!" Joe pretended to wipe the sweat off his brow. "How do you think we're doing so far, Dana?"

They'd cleared a wide strip on either side of this section of the original dilapidated line of fencing and the first few upright poles were already in place.

"Fantastic," I was genuinely impressed. "You've done a lot already."

"There's still a long way to go," Molly's hair was messy and she had a streak of dirt on her face. "But we'll get there!"

"Lucy and I have been marking the trees we want to cut down," Uncle James told me. "She says it'll make the house much lighter."

112

"And you're bringing in a builder to fix the roof, aren't you?" Lucy smiled when she looked at him, and I could see the light of pleasure in Joe's eyes as he watched them both.

"I'll want a good price, of course," the old man said firmly. "And if he does a good job I might think about having the kitchen and bathrooms done."

I laughed with them, and then said diffidently, "I hope it's OK but I kind of took you up on your offer to use that field around the back."

"Of course, of course," Uncle James looked in his benevolent way at Lucy. "I told you your friends are always welcome."

"You mean Page and *Evan* are coming over?" she looked at me in surprise.

"Yeah," I said, acting cool. "I called Evan and suggested we carry on with the training here."

She grinned delightedly and gave me a bear hug. "Nice one, Dana!"

Her parents and uncle looked mildly bewildered at her enthusiasm, but we didn't bother giving them the whole bullying story because adults always freak out at the word *bully* and say you should have told them.

"You've worked wonders with your uncle," I said as my friend and I strolled back to the house, "It's like he's had a personality transplant."

"He's just happy," she said simply. "Getting along with people instead of disagreeing with everyone or chasing them off. Which I must say I think was hugely the fault of that creep Mervyn. Look, I know you don't like secrets, but here's another one for you. Mervyn's accident was actually my uncle's fault. Uncle James told me he feels so guilty because he didn't check properly when he was backing the car out one day."

"So that's the story behind the car accident," I whistled thoughtfully. "I bet Mervyn is taking advantage of his injuries, and all that whining he does is to keep Uncle James feeling guilty."

"Absolutely!" she was so pleased I saw it that way. "That's exactly why the poor old man is putting up with Mervyn's nasty ways, I think. It just isn't fair, because, underneath it all, the real Uncle James is a total sweetie-pie."

The total sweetie-pie was a bit of a pain in the morning, having decided to assist us in our jump building. Evan and Page arrived quite early and though the atmosphere was slightly tense and unnatural to begin with we soon got back into the easy-going, friendly relationship we'd enjoyed before. At first Polar was definitely jittery, obviously rattled by the scare Nick had given him, so I started off with some low fences, a few planks balanced on chairs, raising them up to oil-drum height when the white horse relaxed and began sailing over them with consummate ease. Evan was responsible for the horse's improvement of course, determinedly showing no sign of nerves at all and demonstrating a gritty determination that made his riding better than ever.

"We're going to need more challenging fences," I said, and Uncle James swung into action, dragging us off to a shed that was full of ancient banister rails, flooring planks, old gate, fence panels – in fact everything the amateur course builder could possibly need. I worked my socks off all morning, dragging heavy lengths of wood around to construct a good, varied and adaptable course in the quiet field that was situated near the back of the house. Mervyn rolled his chair out of the kitchen door a few times and glanced briefly in our direction but thankfully didn't come over. The sweat was actually dripping off me once I'd finished pacing out and building, and I told the others I'd take a quick shower before riding Scarlet around the course.

"If you just want to take a break, Polar and I will go first," Evan, all eager and confident again, offered.

"No, I want to make sure I've got all the distances right," I said. "I don't want anything to put Polar off jumping."

To my great satisfaction I'd gotten the course absolutely dead on and, though suitably challenging, it rode really well. Scarlet put in an effortless clear round and Polar, though he struggled a bit with the parallel, managed a very creditable first round, only knocking one pole off and clouting the gate.

"Eight faults!" Evan made a face. "Not exactly a winning tally."

"You let him flatten over the parallel and didn't give him time to look at the gate," I said. "You can work on that, but the main thing is you've got him beautifully balanced and full of confidence."

"Thanks to you," he gave me the grin that still melted my insides. "I honestly didn't realize just how much Polar reacts to the way I'm feeling, but now that you've told me, it's the main thing I'm going to work on."

They spent the whole day at Cornell Hall, resting Polar and Blade in the paddock between training sessions while the four of us hung out in my favorite spot – the old oak tree.

"She's like a manic monkey when she climbs this thing," Lucy grumbled. "I refuse to go any higher than the

115

nice safe fork in the trunk, but Dana would be hanging by her toes from the top branch if you let her!"

To my surprise Evan was a pretty nimble climber himself, and we left the other two half way up and swung our way to the cool, leafy branches higher up.

"It's a great view from up here," I said, peering out toward the brooding line of the prairie, but when Evan replied, "Gorgeous!" I realized he was looking at me.

"Cheesy!" I laughed but I knew I was blushing and I also knew I was thrilled to pieces.

The training went really well too but at the end of the day we were all completely wasted, especially me.

"You look as if you could sleep for a week," Evan gently pushed the hair out of my eyes. "I've never seen anyone work so hard, and I appreciate it – and so does my horse."

Polar blew down his nose in agreement and I managed a last, weary smile before watching the horses and riders walk slowly away down the drive. I slept even more deeply than ever that night and when I woke it was to find Lucy's bed empty, though still ruffled and unmade.

"Luce?" blearily I staggered to my feet and looked around for her.

I took a nearly cold shower to wake myself up and by the time my friend came back my eyes were at least open and my brain just about working.

"Oh Dana," she looked on the verge of tears. "I'm really sorry."

"What for? Oh no, it's not Scarlet? Has something happened to Scarlet?"

"No, she's fine. I've been over and checked them both thoroughly and they haven't been touched."

116

"Haven't been touched? What do you mean?" I stared at her. "Why would –?"

"It's your jumping course. Nick – well, *somebody's* been here at night and smashed it all up."

"Somebody! Yeah, right!" I ran for the door. "It's *got* be that low-life bully!"

The field, which yesterday had looked like an eccentric but totally effective show jumping ring was now a complete and utter mess. My course had been totally trashed, every fence dismantled and thrown around so the whole area was a litter of poles, planks and fence panels.

"Uncle James found it and he came to tell us," Lucy put her arm around me. "Only you slept through all his yelling. He says not much is actually broken – they probably tried not to make too much noise – and we can probably build it up again."

"What's the point?" I said dully. "Nick will only keep trashing it again. Until Evan straightens him out, Nick will just keep following him around doing it for fun, so what exactly is the point?"

"Hey, come on," Lucy hugged me comfortingly. "That doesn't sound like you!"

"It's the way I feel. You'd better tell Page and Evan not to bother coming over. Oh – unless Uncle James wants us to clear the field of all this mess."

"No he said to leave it. I think he understood how upset you'd be and suggested we take a day off from riding altogether, maybe go into Cornell and see a movie or something."

"If you want," I said. I just didn't care.

117

Chapter TEN

I could see Lucy was worrying about me, and when, less than half an hour later, Joe dropped us off at our friends' house, I knew instantly that Evan was deeply concerned too. Being Evan, he couldn't find any words of course, but his body language spoke volumes, and when he put his arm silently around me and pulled me to him I could feel his heartbeat racing frantically. The four of us had still not told the adults the full story of Nick's bullying tactics and they were all assuming the destruction of the jumping course had been done by local kids getting back at Uncle James. Susan, Evan and Page's mother, wanted to call the police but Joe disagreed.

"My uncle doesn't want them involved and I think we'd only be wasting their time anyway. Unfortunately he's had a long running feud with what he thinks are trespassers and I can't believe the police would do much even if we did bother them."

"I suppose so," Susan said, looking doubtful. "Though it does seem dreadful letting somebody get away with such wanton destruction. It's a pity Polar refuses to jump in that schooling ring of ours, because then none of this would have happened."

I personally thought it was about time she knew about Nick and his bullying but Evan, wrapped once again in a dark, shuttered secrecy, was obviously not going to tell her so the rest of us kept our mouths shut too. We hung around for a couple of hours, playing a half-hearted game of tennis, followed by an equally apathetic bout of PlayStation until Susan got fed up with us.

"Go and *do* something," she told her son, "instead of sulking around here all day."

"I want to see a movie," Lucy said, still trying to raise our spirits. "A comedy, or maybe a romance."

Page responded by sticking her fingers down her throat and pretending to gag.

"OK then," Lucy's eyes lit up. "Shopping. Evan can watch us girls indulge in a serious bout of retail therapy."

"We can't do that to my poor brother. I know – bowling!" Page was trying hard too. "There's a bowling alley on the other side of Cornell."

I wanted to scream and yell, *What about Nick? Why aren't we tracking him down and giving him payback?* but Evan said dully, "All right. I don't mind."

"Bowling it is, then," Page said, and turned to Susan. "You don't mind giving us a lift, do you, Mom?"

"Anything if it'll cheer Evan up and stop his moping around," she said, clearly as exasperated with him as I was.

As you might expect, bowling was not a success. Lucy and Page did their best but they were severely handicapped by the two gloomy, silent miseries that were Evan and me. Lucy had arranged for her dad to pick us up at two o'clock, during his *fencing* break, so we still had a lot of time to kill when we left the bowling alley to walk the short distance to the center of town. We got some food, then wandered around the shopping mall for a while, still avoiding the subject of the destroyed jumping course. Totally fed up, I left the other three and took off to have one more look at the super-cool shoe shop and, while I half-heartedly ogled those wedges, I suddenly saw Nick's sneering face reflected in the shop window. I spun around and knew my eyes were blazing.

"Hello gorgeous," he smiled insolently. "Glad to see me?"

"Oh yeah," I purred nastily. "There's nothing I like more than meeting up with the local moron."

His face darkened and he made a sudden grab at my wrist. "You got no manners, do you know that? You need to be taught a lesson."

Quick as a flash I jabbed him hard in the ribs with my free hand, stomping down on his foot at the same time. Hissing with pain, he roared loudly and jumped back but he didn't let go of my arm, pulling me savagely away from the shop window. I tried to struggle free, kicking and hitting him but he kept walking and he kept dragging me with him. Several people shook their heads and looked annoyed, but I guess they thought it was just rough kids fooling around, so no one intervened. It wasn't until I realized that Nick was hauling me toward one of the exits that I started to feel scared, and as I twisted and tried to pull away I let out a piercing scream. His response was immediate, yanking my arm so hard I thought it would break and slamming me against a wall in the quiet, nearly deserted corner of the exit aisle.

"Shut up!" he said, and then called me a horrible name and put his big, sweaty hand across my mouth while pinning me against the wall so I couldn't move to hit or kick at him.

It was one of the few times in my life I've been truly frightened, so you can imagine how I felt when a deep, familiar voice said, "Get off her *now!*" and Nick was hoisted upward and sideways, forcing him to release his grip at last.

I staggered a little, wiping at my mouth in disgust to remove the smell and feel of his hand. I looked back at the

tall, furious figure of Evan who now had Nick in a vice-like hold further along the wall.

"I'll – I'll call Security," I gasped and he turned his blonde head to look at me.

"No, I'll take care of this myself. Are you all right?"

"Oh, yes," even though I still felt a bit sick, I managed to smile. "I'm all right now."

Lucy and Page, running pretty fast, arrived behind me and Page let out a squeal when she saw her brother and Nick.

"It's all right," I put a hand on her arm. "Don't call anyone – Evan wants to do this on his own."

"You're as white as a sheet, Dana," Lucy put her arm around me. "Come and sit down, and we'll get you a drink."

They both fussed over me, but though I did genuinely feel shaky, I was also aware of a wonderful warm glow flooding through me. Evan took quite a while *taking care of* Nick, but when he walked back toward me he looked two feet taller and ten times as handsome without the hunched, wary demeanor he'd had before.

"You sure you're OK?" he sat down beside me and took my hand.

"Yeah. I – I'm sorry I tried to tackle Nick on my own. It was a stupid thing to do."

"Thank goodness you let out that yell," he said and his arm tightened around me. "We had no idea where you'd gone."

"So, what did Nick say?" Page was agog. "Did you get him to swear he'd quit sabotaging your training and trashing any more jumps?"

"He definitely won't be bothering us again," Evan said with quiet confidence. "Dana was right, the guy's a piece of nothing if you stand up to him."

I squeezed the hand that still held mine. "What was it all about, then –this whole campaign trying to stop your riding?"

"It wasn't as specific as that. It just boils down to jealousy. Nick sees me as some spoiled rich kid who's got everything. Seems he resents that and started jeering at Polar and me as a joke, but when he found I was an easy target he just kept going."

"He's like most bullies. He picks on people he knows he can trample on," I said. "And I'm including myself in that. He's physically a lot bigger and stronger than I am, and I don't mind admitting he scared the life out of me."

"Well he won't ever scare you again," Evan's mouth was set in a determined line.

"And presumably he won't trash any more of Dana's courses," Lucy put in. "Or trespass at Cornell Hall, for that matter."

A frown creased Evan's forehead. "The one thing Nick *is* denying is being responsible for last night. He says he just liked turning up at my practices and scaring Polar into throwing me."

"Oh yeah – what's he trying to do – pretend there's some other bully boy who just *happened* to bust up the fences we built?" Page didn't believe a word of it.

"Well, he did point out that he's never destroyed any of our stuff before," Evan said, clearly puzzled. "The way he put it was 'If I trashed your fences I wouldn't get the fun of scaring your horse into dumping you, would I?'"

"This time was different, though, wasn't it, because he knew he wouldn't be able to get near your training session now that you were doing it at my uncle's place," Lucy said, of the same

123

opinion as Page. "Of course it was Nick, but if you've – um – *convinced* him not to do it again, what the heck?"

"Oh I've convinced him all right," Evan said grimly. "And from now on if Dana wants me to use our ring then that's where we'll be. Now that I've stopped being such a sap we can go wherever we like."

"You might have to work hard to convince Polar of that," I smiled at him. "He still needs a lot of confidence building."

"We've got a long time for you both to work on him," Lucy said happily. "My mom and dad will be working on that fence for at least two weeks, I bet."

"And then there are all the other improvements you and your uncle have planned," I teased her.

"I know. Maybe once Uncle James has told them about the you-know-what, we'll be staying even longer!"

"I'm all for that," Evan's voice was eager. "Only what's a you-know-what?"

"Ooh," Lucy said, clapping a hand to her mouth. "I'm not supposed to say anything, am I, Dana?"

"No, it's a deep, dark Harmon family secret," I laughed.

"I'll tell you all about it once my parents know," Lucy promised a slightly bemused looking Page. "And, oh look – it's two o'clock – we have to go and meet them."

As we ran out of the shopping mall I thought how surprised Joe would be by the change in Evan and me. When he'd left us with Susan a few hours earlier we'd both been wrapped in gloom, whereas now, still holding Evan's hand, I felt I was about to burst with happiness. As we clambered into the car I turned a beaming face toward Joe – and stopped in surprise. His own normally smiling expression had changed as dramatically as mine.

124

"What's the matter, Dad?" Lucy was staring at him. "You look – weird."

"I feel weird," he said shortly. "I'll tell you about it when we get home. Um – Evan, do you mind if I drop you and Page off first? There's been – something's happened back at Cornell Hall that the family has to discuss."

"Oh sure," Evan raised his eyebrows. "It's nothing to do with last night, is it?"

"Last night? What do you mean?" Joe asked sharply.

"The way our jump course was trashed. I wondered if Mr. Harmon is worrying about who did it, because –"

"No, no, it's a lot more serious than a bunch of hooligans breaking up your fences," Joe was looking very grim.

Lucy, sitting beside him in the front seat, started hissing questions, and by the time the car drew up outside Evan's and Page's house she, too, was looking deeply disturbed.

"See you later," Page said cheerfully as she got out. "Hope everything's OK."

Lucy turned a shocked face and said, "No it's not, but I'll try and call you."

"What happened?" I leaned forward as we turned down the road leading to the Hall. "Is someone sick?"

Joe made the short, barking sound of a pretend laugh. "Maybe that's it, maybe my uncle is mentally ill – who can say?"

"Dad's upset because something horrible happened this morning," Lucy turned to look at me. "Someone broke in and stole something from Uncle James's study."

"No, Lucy, you didn't understand what I said. There *was* no break-in – the police have been in and they're very clear about that. The necklace, according to my uncle, simply vanished from a room he himself had locked."

"The necklace?" It was the first time I had heard Joe mention it.

"It's a long and complicated story," he said now. "But the gist of the matter is that Uncle James kept a valuable piece of jewelry locked in his study. This morning, while Molly and I were working with the digger, my uncle went to the room and discovered it was gone. By his own admission the door was firmly locked, using the only key which is kept in his possession at all times, and when he checked the window it was properly locked from the inside as well. So, given that information, are you at all surprised that the police have already left, telling us that there has been no break in and that they cannot treat the disappearance as a burglary?"

"So what *are* they treating it as?" I looked at him in bewilderment as he swung the car up Cornell Hall's drive.

"A rather pleasant policewoman suggested to me, very gently, that perhaps my uncle had mislaid the thing himself. 'He's quite elderly,' she told me, 'and often the elderly are forgetful, putting stuff back in the wrong place and getting in a muddle.'"

"That could be true, couldn't it?" I said hopefully.

"Does that sound like a description of Uncle James?" Joe's voice was full of suppressed anger. "Yes, he's getting old, but he's still as sharp as a tack. This is just the latest in his campaign to deprive Lucy of something that should be hers by birthright."

"My great-grandmother's necklace, you mean?" Lucy said coolly and he brought the car to a sudden, shuddering halt.

126

"You knew about the necklace?" he stared at her incredulously. "How?"

"Uncle James told me. He showed me the Helena Harmon portrait and took the necklace from his desk and told me it would be mine when I was twenty-one."

"That's what he said to me," Joe still looked dazed. "But he only told me he intended you having it *after* he claimed it had been stolen. I mean, I had no idea the thing was in the house. I always assumed it would be in a safe or a bank vault – the kind of place a normal person would keep it!"

"Don't keep saying Uncle James isn't normal! You obviously don't believe his story about the theft," Lucy sounded really angry. "Why not?"

"I told you – the police found absolutely no sign of a break in and your uncle swears he had the only key, so what am I supposed to think?"

"What about Mervyn?" Lucy asked bluntly. "He could have made a copy of the key."

"No, he's out of the picture completely – look, we'll go in the house and your Mom will go through the whole story. She's calmer than I am. I've gotten myself worked up and in a real state because Uncle James is refusing to discuss it sanely."

"He doesn't know how to handle confrontation, and just can't find the right words, so he clams up," Lucy said impatiently. "But I don't believe he'd have told you a pack of lies, so let's find out exactly how it all happened."

It was true, Molly was calmer than her husband but she still looked pretty upset.

"Kay's still at the hospital with Mervyn. She phoned just now and said they're letting him come home, but he'll have to stay in bed for a few days," she greeted Joe before grabbing Lucy and hugging her tight.

"What? Why?" Lucy extricated herself. "Oh Mom, sit down and start at the beginning – Dad's told us half a story and I don't know what the heck's going on."

"Lucy knows about the necklace – she'll tell you about that in a minute," Joe said, filling the kettle at the sink.

"Right," Molly said and took a deep breath. "Here goes. Uncle James says he unlocked his study this morning and went in there with Kay so she could give it the weekly cleaning. While they were in there they heard a tremendous crash and Mervyn screaming. They rushed straight to him, though your uncle insists he firmly re-locked the study door. Mervyn was trapped behind the door of the bathroom in their quarters. He'd fallen out of his chair which had tipped up and was blocking the doorway so they couldn't get in to help him right away."

"Was he conscious?" Lucy asked.

"Yes, Kay was talking to him the whole time, trying to get him to move away from the door so they could force it open. They didn't dare slam into it, in case they injured Mervyn even more. After a while, a few minutes or so, Mervyn managed to crawl out of the way and they were able to get in and help him. He said he was all right but Kay insisted she take him to hospital to get him checked over – they've got a specially adapted car to take the wheelchair."

"So, when did the necklace disappear? I mean, was it during all this or could it have gone missing earlier?" I was listening closely.

"Your uncle can pinpoint it exactly, and says it was

128

stolen between him and Kay leaving the study and his returning there immediately after she left for the hospital."

"Is he absolutely sure of that?" Lucy was frowning. "Isn't it more likely that whoever got onto the grounds last night and destroyed our jumps also took the necklace while they were here?"

I gaped at her – was she now saying that Nick was not just a bully but a housebreaking jewel thief as well?

"No, though if Uncle James had spent more time working on his story he could have suggested that," Joe said bitterly. "No, according to him he checked the necklace as he did every single time he went into that room. It was there when he locked the door before going to Mervyn's rescue, but when he returned it was gone."

"The window!" Lucy said. "The thief got in through the window."

"Well, you'd think your uncle would have at least left an element of possibility there, but oh no, he's 100% certain it was locked. He said he found the open, empty jewelry case and ran straight to the window to check."

"And it was definitely locked?"

"It can only be fastened from the inside, a sliding lock you pull across –impossible to open from the outside." Joe raised his hands in despair. "No wonder the police didn't stay long. They took statements from us, of course, but we were over by the new fence with the digger the whole morning so we couldn't help. They'll interview Mervyn, I suppose, but I can tell you now what they're thinking. This is either, like the policewoman said, a case of a forgetful old man getting in a muddle or –" he stopped and I said tentatively, "Or?"

"My dad thinks Uncle James is making it all up, don't you, Dad?" Lucy's chin was tilted defiantly.

Joe looked at her sadly. "I'm sorry, hon, I know you're getting fond of him but yes, I think this is just another way of your uncle avoiding handing over Helena's necklace to you. As far as I'm concerned I've *had* it with him. We're getting out of here as soon as we can and I for one am never *ever* coming back!"

Chapter ELEVEN

Totally selfish I know, but my first reaction wasn't, *Oh poor Lucy*, but, *oh poor me*. Being told the uncle she's growing fonder of each day is a scheming old devil intent on cheating her out of a family heirloom is HUGE, so I gave myself a shake and tried not to think that it meant I probably wouldn't see Evan again.

I put my arm around my friend and gave her a gentle hug to say how sorry I was, but I don't think she noticed.

"Don't be dumb!" she snapped, glaring at Joe who took a step back in surprise. "Uncle James *wants* me to have my great-grandmother's necklace. He always intended I should have it and he's even more determined now that he's met me."

"Lucy, honey," Molly said, unaccustomed to these passionate outbursts from her daughter. "You can't have been listening. The story your uncle has concocted is – well, pure nonsense."

"Doesn't that prove he's telling the truth? Uncle James is pretty smart. Wouldn't he have come up with something far more convincing?"

Molly and Joe looked at each other.

"It was probably a spur of the moment decision," Joe said. "He was upset by Mervyn's fall and decided to put a half-formulated idea into action. I think he always intended keeping the necklace as a kind of insurance for his old age."

"You said he already has plenty of money," Lucy said, with color on her cheekbones as she fought for her corner. "So why would he decide today that he needs more?"

Joe shrugged helplessly. "I don't know, maybe the

131

thought of losing Mervyn and Kay if the fall was a bad one. I don't pretend to understand the workings of the man's peculiar mind but I am convinced he never intended letting you have his mother's necklace."

"So, despite being perfectly intelligent he suddenly invents a robbery no one is going to believe in?" Lucy just would *not* let it go.

"Well, maybe not so sudden. He was eager to get you out of the house this morning – who knows, maybe he even destroyed those jumps of yours to make sure you wouldn't stay around."

I heard Lucy's furious intake of breath and knew that despite herself she was thinking about Nick's vehement denial. "You can't believe that. He's basically a good, kind man. I know he puts on a grumpy, bad tempered act but he'd *never* do anything dishonest and cruel like this."

"I'm sorry," Joe said and shook his head. "I've known him a lot longer than you have and I don't think any of that's true. I seriously believe he's mean and twisted. I came here with a genuine desire to help an old man and let bygones be bygones, but I can't take any more. Helena's necklace should have been yours, and the fact that my uncle didn't even bother making the story of a theft convincing shows how little he cares for us – particularly you."

"No!" Lucy's eyes were blazing. "It's not true. Someone else stole that necklace. It wasn't my Uncle James!"

"The police say –" Molly began but Lucy wouldn't listen any more.

"I don't care, I don't care what the police or any of you say – it wasn't him!"

She turned and ran then, out of the kitchen through the

132

back door, her blonde hair streaming behind her as she passed the kitchen window.

"Oh boy!" Molly groaned. "I didn't expect this! What are we going to do with her?"

"There's nothing we can do," Joe spoke with finality. "We're leaving, and that's all there is to it."

"Um – when?" I was hovering around awkwardly, not sure what to do. "I mean, do you want me to pack or should I go and talk to Lucy or –"

"That would be good," Molly forced a smile. "She must be feeling so hurt by her uncle's treachery."

But Lucy, when I found her at the old oak tree, was still spitting defiance.

"I just don't believe it," she'd scrambled up to the broad fork of the trunk. "Someone else did the stealing."

"But the room was locked, both the door and the window. No one broke in, and he *says* that Mervyn and Kay, who might just possibly have a key, were with your uncle during the whole time he says the necklace went missing."

"Don't go *he says*, like that! You don't believe he's innocent either!"

"I'm really sorry, but I don't see how he can be." I tried to defend myself. "No one broke in, your mom and dad were with the digger, you and I were with Page and Evan, and Kay was with your uncle while they both tried to rescue Mervyn from his fall, so who else is there?"

"I don't know," her voice was sulky. "A passing hiker or – ooh I know, your precious Spy Man!"

"I guess he could have been around, but there's still no way he could have gotten into that room, and anyway how would he know that there was valuable jewelry in the desk?

133

Like your dad said, anyone normal would have kept the necklace in a safe."

"Oh, so you agree as well that my uncle isn't normal?" The bright flashes of color were back on Lucy's cheekbones. "Well thanks, Dana. What a real good, loyal friend you turned out to be!"

I watched helplessly as she turned her head, pointedly ignoring me, and wished harder than I ever have before that I could *do* something to help her. Everything had looked so promising for the rest of our stay and now it had all gone wrong. I took off for the horses' paddock and had a long cuddle with Scarlet, telling her all about our problems. When my cell phone rang it made us both jump, and when I heard Evan's voice I nearly cried.

"What is it? What's the matter, Dana?" He was concerned and I tried hard to pull myself together.

"It's too complicated, but – oh Evan, I don't think I'll be seeing you again. Lucy's parents want to go home."

"No! Oh no! When?"

"More or less right away." The tears were prickling behind my eyelids again.

"At least let me say goodbye," he said, sounding as upset as I was. "I'll come over –"

"You'd better not," I rubbed my eyes fiercely. "We've got serious trouble here. Look, I'll ride Scarlet and meet you up in the woods – in the clearing. They won't go without me, and at least this way our horses will get to see each other one more time as well."

"OK. I'll wait for you."

I ran off to get Scarlet's tack and got her ready immediately. Within a few minutes we were riding out of the old gateway toward the sandy trail. Just as we were about to turn toward the woods I looked back at Cornell Hall for what I told myself might be the last time – and froze. There, binoculars in hand, was Mr. Spy Man, just about to climb over the fence onto the grounds.

"Hey!" I let out a yell and he instantly jumped back down again and started running toward the prairie.

We were quite a distance away, giving him a good start, but this time nothing was going to keep me from chasing him. Maybe Lucy was right and he was the thief! I figured if I could get him to confess and prove that her faith in her uncle was justified, she'd realize I'd been rooting for her all along. Even as I put Scarlet into a gallop I knew I could be riding into danger, but my friend needed all the help she could get and I was determined to give it my all.

"If this guy gives us any trouble we can always yell for help," I told my pony. "We should catch up with him before he's gone beyond the fence, and they'll be able to hear us in the house."

But, to my surprise and disappointment there was no sign of the man as we thundered along the upward slope to the prairie.

"No one runs *that* fast," I cantered to the top of the humpbacked hill and looked around me. "There he is!" I pointed and Scarlet's intelligent ears flickered in the same direction. "He's got a bike!"

The bike was really traveling fast as the man pedaled furiously away from the Hall, and I knew I had to follow. I also knew some of the trails were too narrow and twisting to take at a gallop, so we set off at a good working canter, keeping the moving figure clearly in sight. I was concentrating so hard on making sure we didn't lose him that at first I didn't notice the change in the prairie around us. It wasn't until we had to slow down to negotiate a tricky bend that I realized we were now surrounded by the sickly acid green of marsh plants growing right up to the edge of the trail. Ahead, Mr. Spy Man kept going, weaving his way expertly through the boggy path in a way that told me he'd taken this route many times before.

By following his exact trail, Scarlet and I managed to get through every twist and turn without once stepping off the trail into the dangerous sinking mud of the marsh, and I kept praying our luck would hold. At last the sandy path beneath us widened, the marsh plants gave way to a vigorous growth of prairie grasses and I knew we were back on safe ground, though exactly *where* I had no idea. There was, of course, the small factor of tackling the unknown bike rider but I figured I'd worry about that when it happened. It happened almost immediately, in fact. As we turned the next bend we could see, on a patch of coarse grass, a small tent and, flung down beside it, the mountain bike we'd been following. I brought Scarlet to a halt and looked nervously around.

The tent flap moved and a head looked out. "Wow, I've been running away from a kid!"

"Excuse me?" I said, trying to muster up some dignity. "I'm not a kid, and anyway I'm not alone – my friend's coming and he's – um – a lot older."

"Friend?" he came out of the tent and I was glad to see he was small and skinny. "Not that psychopath in the wheelchair? The one who won't let me near the Hall?"

"Mervyn?" This interview wasn't going exactly the way I'd hoped. "No, not him, but that's kind of why I – I mean my friend and I – are here. Because of the way you keep spying on us."

"You live at Cornell Hall? I've seen you there, of course, but I didn't know there were any kids actually living there."

"I'm staying there with my friend and I've seen you watching us with binoculars and trespassing on the grounds."

"Yeah, well I'm sorry about that. I did ask very politely if I could get inside but that psycho – sorry, Mervyn – threatened to chase me off with a gun. Not exactly a reasonable sort of guy, so I took drastic measures and hoped he wouldn't find out."

"I don't blame Mervyn for chasing you with his gun," I lied. "I mean – spying on people like that –"

"I'm *not* spying," he said indignantly. "I'm only trying to record a rare sighting."

I stared at him blankly.

"Of a bird. I'm a birdwatcher. I've been here for weeks because there's a rare migrant on the prairie; I won't bore you with its name. Unfortunately it now seems to have settled somewhere in the trees around Cornell Hall, so that's why I've been creeping around in there."

"Bird watching?" It's not something I *get,* to be honest. "Oh. I thought, when I chased you, well I was trying to solve a mystery for my friend back there and I thought you could help."

"Is something going on at the Hall?" he asked curiously. "I've certainly seen some weird goings on, so I wondered."

"What goings on? What have you seen?" I leaned forward eagerly.

The bird watcher, Ken, in trying to record his elusive rare bird, had spent a lot of time over the last few days inside the grounds, his binoculars trained on the trees crowding in on the old house. Apart from being crazy about birds, he seemed really nice and gave a wonderful, succinct rundown of all the *goings on* he'd mentioned. At first I listened in disbelief, but as a clear picture emerged I realized exactly what had happened during the time of the theft and knew without a doubt who the culprit was.

"That's just what I wanted," I was nearly incoherent with excitement. "Thank you so much, Ken. Are you sure you're willing to talk about what you saw with anyone else who needs to know?"

"Sure, here's my phone number," he handed it over. "Though if you want to wait until I've had something to eat I'll come back to the Hall with you."

"No, it's OK," I said. I was so anxious to get back and tell Lucy what I'd discovered I wasn't thinking straight. "I need to go right away."

"Stick to the same trail then," he warned. "But I guess you know your way across the marsh as well as I do."

Well, no, I thought. *I don't actually, but it'll be simple if I take exactly the same route, won't it?*

Yeah, you've guessed it, within a few minutes of leaving the bird watcher's tent the *simple* plan had backfired. I had absolutely no idea which trail I'd followed him along and knew we were in deep, deep trouble.

"OK," I said, pulling Scarlet up and trying not to panic as I looked around desperately for a familiar landmark.

The prairie rolled away into the distance as ever but there seemed to be no end to the expanse of yellowish green indicating boggy marshland, and the narrow trail beneath us now forked into three separate trails.

"We're lost," I told my pony. "I think we should have turned left back there instead of going straight."

She snorted, which could have signified agreement but was more likely her way of telling me what a fool she thought I was.

"If we turn really carefully," I cautiously edged her around, "we can go back and take the right trail."

Scarlet, doing her best to perform a perfect forehand turn, slipped slightly and her near hind leg dropped suddenly into the oozing mud at the side of the trail. I dismounted immediately, grabbing her leg in both hands and hauling upwards to help it back on dry land. Scarlet was really good, not panicking or struggling, which would have made things far worse. Even when she was safe again I found I was still trembling. At that point it would have been a good idea to call Ken and ask for his help but, still desperate to get back with the astounding information he'd given me, I stupidly decided to keep going. I rode my pony carefully back to the last fork in the trail and this time took the left hand trail, wishing with all my heart I'd been blessed with a decent sense of direction.

This time, though, it seemed I got it right. The trail, though narrow and twisting, seemed perfectly solid and appeared to be winding its way out of the boggy marsh. Again my eagerness to get back overcame common sense and instead of taking it at a steady walk, I put Scarlet into canter. I can only say I must have been communicating my nervousness in a spectacular fashion because, when a sudden gust of wind blew some dead gorse so it went tumbling across the trail, my usually bomb-proof horse slammed on the brakes and stopped so suddenly she threw me violently over her head. I landed on the soft, yielding mass of marsh plants and for a blind, idiotic moment I thought I was safe. It wasn't until I tried to move that I realized I was sinking, slowly but inexorably into the mud. The more I moved the deeper I sank, and within moments I was up to my waist in thick, slimy ooze with the safety of the dry trail out of reach of my shaking, outstretched fingers.

Chapter TWELVE

Scarlet, after a first frightened, panicky run, had stayed nearby, her head turned toward me as if looking in great puzzlement. The phone I should have used earlier was in my pocket under the mud, out of reach and no doubt ruined and useless now.

"Scarlet!" I called urgently. "Go and find help! Go back to the tent and bring Ken!"

Yeah I know, I sounded like someone from one of those old Lassie films, but what else could I do? I tried moving forward again and immediately felt the sinking sensation as the mud sucked and dragged at my legs.

"Go on, Scarlet!" I was screaming now. "Just go!"

She tossed her head, sending her reins flapping and took off, cantering neatly between the menacing lines of marsh plants. I tried hard to breathe slowly and calmly and not move a muscle. The birdwatcher's tent, I figured, wasn't too far away but I had no idea whether Scarlet would remember the route. I refused to think about the option that my pony had no more idea than I did of where we were or which way to go, because if I started to imagine her lost and frightened in this horrible, scary world of the marsh I would have broken down completely. The mud, I have to tell you, was DISGUSTING, thick, slimy and clinging, and the thought of it closing over my head, filling nose and mouth, was just too gross for words. In between yelling to let anyone know where I was, I tried to think of other things, concentrating hard on the extraordinary story Ken had told me, to make the time go quicker. Later, I realized I was actually only in that bog for ten minutes or so, but it felt like forever!

The first glorious sign I was going to be OK was the sound of a voice calling, "Dana, hang in there, we're coming," followed by the smooth rhythm of cantering hooves. I squinted into the sun and there, coming toward me, was Evan riding his stunning white horse, the pair of them rimmed with light so they glowed like heroes in a Hollywood movie. Evan was leading Scarlet and I almost burst into tears of relief and thankfulness that not only was my pony unharmed, but that she really had brought me my rescuer.

"Whoa," Evan said and slowed them both to walk, approaching me slowly and carefully. "OK, Dana, I'm going to reach out and get your hand. You'll need to hold tight and kick with your legs like you're swimming under water."

"I might pull you in too!" I was numb with fright.

"No you won't. I'll use Polar's strength to drag you out."

Looping the reins around one hand, he stretched out the other toward me, inching toward me until I could grab it with both hands. The vile mud sucked and pulled at my legs as I tried to move them. but gradually, gradually Evan and Polar won, dragging me further and further through the marsh until at last I was lying on the wonderful firm safety of the trail. I coughed and spluttered, and then rolled onto my back and looked up.

"Oh," I said stupidly. "Poor Scarlet's got a black leg!"

Evan burst out laughing and helped me gently to my feet. "Whereas you have a black everything, more or less."

I looked down at the thick slime plastered all over my lower body and liberally splashed on chest, arms and probably face and shook my head. "I'm really sorry. Thank you so much for rescuing me."

"Not me," he grinned and wiped some mud off my nose. "Polar. When we saw Scarlet charging across the prairie with a muddy leg and no rider I knew you must have fallen off in the marsh but I didn't think I could get my horse in there to find you. He was totally amazing, and cantered through the middle of it as though he's never been scared of the place in his life."

"It was you," I climbed squelchily into my saddle. "You gave him the confidence to be a hero."

On the way back Evan explained how he'd hung around waiting for me at the clearing in the woods until, worried out of his mind, he'd gone to find me.

"You didn't try to call me?" I looked sadly at my now ruined phone.

"No. You said there was serious trouble so I knew that if you'd gotten involved it would be difficult to talk. But," he gave me *that* look, "I couldn't stand the thought of you leaving so I rode over and snuck up the drive."

"Did you see anyone to ask?"

"Not a soul, but I checked the paddock and saw that Scarlet was gone. I'd just ridden through the woods so I knew you weren't there and the prairie seemed like an obvious choice."

"I'm really sorry I didn't call and tell you where I was going, but it all happened so fast," I smiled at him, hoping I didn't look like a complete wreck. "I'm so lucky you came looking for me."

"If anyone sees you in your current state, lucky isn't the word they'd use to describe you!" He leaned over and wiped another lump of mud off my face.

A thought struck me. "I don't suppose you'd keep on rescuing me by taking care of my poor black legged pony, would you? I *have* to talk to my friend and her family."

"Of course I will," he said and grinned again. "But urgent or not, you should maybe take a shower first."

I managed to get upstairs without leaving mud trails everywhere, as the stuff had started to dry and harden in the sun. The easiest way to deal with the mess I was in was to step into the shower, clothes and all, and let the vile mud be washed completely down the drain. It was very quiet everywhere and I eventually tracked down Joe, Molly and Lucy at the old oak tree.

"Lucy's up there and she won't come down," Joe was standing helplessly at the foot of the tree. "She won't pack, she won't get Petal ready, and she won't even talk to us."

"Lucy, I'm coming up," I climbed swiftly up to the broad branch where my friend sat, arms folded, chin tilted.

"If you've come to persuade me to leave you can forget it," she greeted me. "I'm not leaving Cornell Hall until the *real* necklace thief is found."

"Well then, you're in luck," I said amicably. "That's just what I'm about to reveal, so I think you'll want to come down and watch me do it."

"What?" she looked at me suspiciously. "It's a trick. You're on my mom and dad's side, aren't you?"

"I'm on *your* side, Luce, and I always have been, so come on. I've often wondered what it would be like to play that scene where the brilliant detective tells everyone how the crime was committed!"

Still looking slightly unsure, Lucy followed me down

the tree, and before her parents could start talking I held up my hand.

"I want you all to come with me so you can learn exactly what happened here this morning."

We walked across to the house and I marched straight for the back door.

"Shouldn't we go around the front if you want us on our own?" Joe asked, but I shook my head and led them all into the kitchen.

Kay was working as usual while Mervyn slumped in his chair, watching her.

"Didn't the hospital tell you to spend a few days in bed?" I enquired, taking a seat at the big table.

"They recommended it, but there's too much to do around here," he glanced sharply at the Harmon family. "Do you want something?"

"Yeah, a little chat," I said, very assertively. "Where's Uncle James?"

"I'm here," the old man said as he appeared in the doorway. "I thought you were all leaving once you'd persuaded Lucy."

"They can't persuade me," my friend said. Her chin was tilted up, with its familiar air of defiance. "I know you're innocent, Uncle James, and I won't go till my parents know it too."

Her great-uncle looked at her so lovingly it nearly brought a tear to my eye, except of course this was no time for crying.

"Please join us," I showed him to a vacant chair. "I've got something to tell you all."

I started by explaining how I'd seen Ken and chased him

146

across the prairie (omitting the falling off part – that was nothing to boast about, I felt).

"I saw Ken on my first day at Cornell Hall," I said, "and always thought of him as the Spy Man, but in fact the binoculars he's been training on the house and grounds aren't for spying. They're for bird watching."

"So?" Lucy glowered at me.

"So, he's been trying to get a sighting of a rare bird, but what he got this morning was something *really* extraordinary."

"Come on, Dana, spit it out," Joe said. He was feeling uncomfortable, sitting so near the uncle he'd vowed never to speak to again.

"OK. Ken saw the third window on the right at the back of the house open up and someone climb out. He then watched as that person ran around the side of the house and clambered into the second window you come to, reappearing only minutes later. Ken said they had their back to him at that point but they appeared to fiddle around with something, until there was a brief flash of light. Then they ran to the back of the house again where they climbed back into the room they'd come from."

There was complete silence for a moment, and then Molly said tentatively, "I'm very sorry, Dana, but I don't understand what you're saying. Who was this person your birdwatcher saw and what was he or she doing?"

"Oh, it was a he. In fact that's why, after his first sighting, Ken watched so closely. The man in question was someone Ken had seen before. Someone who'd told him to clear off several times and refused to let him enter the grounds to look for the bird."

"Uncle James, you mean?" Flashes of color sprang up on Lucy's face. "You're trying to say Uncle James was up to no good out there, aren't you?"

"No, not your uncle," I smiled at her reassuringly. "Ken was very interested because the man he saw running briskly around the outside of the house was usually *in a wheelchair!*"

"Mervyn?" Joe turned his head and stared at him. "The third window on the right is your bathroom, isn't it?"

"And the second window on the side is my study," Uncle James's voice was raised. "So what on earth –?"

"This is utter nonsense," Mervyn swung his wheelchair to face the old man. "I was lying in agony on the floor of my bathroom – you know that, since you spoke to me."

"But you didn't hear him answer, did you, Uncle James?" I said swiftly. "Oh, you heard Kay pretending to soothe and calm him, and I bet it seemed like she responded to his replies, too."

"She was right up against the door," he said slowly. "Pressed against it so she could hear what he said – but no, you're right, I didn't actually hear his voice."

"No, and that's because *Mervyn wasn't there.*" I felt just like a detective. "It was all a setup. Mervyn wasn't lying on the floor. He was climbing out of the window and running to your office where he climbed through that window, carefully unlocked by Kay when she was cleaning. He shoved the necklace in his pocket and ran back to his bathroom where he finally *managed* to open the door so you'd see him sprawled there groaning with the wheelchair tipped over."

There was another short, stunned silence.

148

"But the study window," Uncle James was staring at me. "When I discovered the necklace was gone, I checked the window and found it locked as it always is."

"Yeah, I don't know how he did that," I admitted. "Ken couldn't see exactly what was happening, but Mervyn fiddled around at the window and there was a flare of light so he must have rigged up something."

"Ken couldn't see!" Mervyn jeered. "What a load of garbage! This Ken, or whatever his real name is, has dreamed up a fantasy story to get you off his back, you stupid girl. It's obvious *he's* the thief. Mr. Harmon knows I can barely stand since the accident he caused, let alone climb and run."

Uncle James flushed guiltily and Lucy went immediately to him and put her arm through his.

Thinking fast I said, "We can soon prove whether that's true. Why don't I just call the hospital? I can ask them about the original accident and the trip you and Kay are *supposed* to have made there this morning."

"Call away," Mervyn tried calling my bluff. "Make a fool of yourself. Why should I care?"

I knew he was trying to freak me out but it still took some effort on my part to start walking across the room to the telephone on the wall.

"Look at her!" Mervyn sounded so sure of himself. "She's hardly using her brain. Just answer me this, Dana, *why* would I go to all that trouble when any time I liked I could just wait for the house to be empty, then smash the study window and pretend we'd had burglars?"

I actually couldn't think of a reply but I picked up the receiver anyway.

"You don't need to make that call," Kay's quiet, flat

voice came almost as a shock. "I'll tell you why my husband set it up the way he did. He *wanted* the family to think Uncle James was lying about the theft, so they'd turn against him and leave. Mervyn knew his cushy life and inheritance ambitions were over now that Mr. Harmon had Joe, Molly and especially Lucy back in his life."

"Shut your mouth!" Mervyn's face was nearly black with anger. "You stupid, stupid woman, just shut up!"

"No, Mervyn, I won't," she said and straightened up with her back against the sink, looking at him with undisguised disgust. "You've done some nasty things in your life, but tearing this nice family apart and breaking Mr. Harmon's heart in the process is more than I can stand."

"Kay? Kay, you knew last year I hadn't injured him?" Uncle James, still arm-in-arm with Lucy, took a step toward her.

She hung her head. "Yes I knew, but I was too afraid to say anything. He had a few bruises and his leg was sore for a few days, but when he saw how guilty you felt he decided to make the most of it."

"So you pretended to be crippled by the accident so you could milk my uncle for his money?" Joe was furious and I saw Mervyn shift uneasily in his chair.

"He's been doing that for years." The formerly monosyllabic Kay couldn't get the words out quickly enough. "He's encouraged Mr. Harmon not to spend and he's made sure we're the only people the old gentleman ever sees so that when the time comes we, well Mervyn, because I'm never given a penny, will get a good fat sum of money. Cornell Hall is entailed to you, of course, but Mervyn made sure no one else was allowed near Mr. Harmon, so we'd be the ones to get the cash. And since the accident, my despicable husband hasn't even had to do a day's work while he waited!"

"That is absolutely shocking!" Molly was aghast as she stared at Mervyn. "You've let this house crumble around Uncle James's ears rather than let him spend any of the money you made sure he'd leave you!"

Mervyn's rat-like features were still livid. "Your family didn't come near him for years, so why shouldn't I get it?"

"I tried to mend the rift many times," Joe said, "But when Uncle James refused to answer my letters I gave up."

"Mr. Harmon never got any letters," Kay said simply. "Mervyn saw to that."

With a cry of frustrated fury the man in the wheelchair leapt to his feet and ran at her, hands outstretched toward her neck. Joe was too quick for him, moving in to block and hitting him with a left hook a prizefighter would be proud of. Staggering back, Mervyn made another lunge, suddenly ducking sideways to run out the back door.

"Don't worry," Kay put out a tentative hand toward Uncle James. "I've got the necklace; I was never going to let him take it. It was just his insurance, really, in case this scheme of his didn't break up your family the way he planned. His main intention was to get rid of them so he could go back to his cushy life of taking every penny he could off you."

"Like the cash I gave him for the operation he said he needed?"

"That's in the bank," she said with a small smile. "But it's in my name; he was scared of having it traced to him. You can have it back, of course – every penny."

"Poor Kay," I said as Lucy squeezed her uncle's arm. "You've been bullied by that man all your life, haven't you?"

"Not any more," Uncle James gave one of his rare, sweet smiles. "Just for once it's Mervyn who'll be chased off, but you're welcome to stay without him, Kay my dear."

"Aren't you going to call the police and tell them what we did?" Kay's eyes were full of tears.

"No, I don't want you involved, so I shall tell them the necklace has been found and let them put me down in their notes as a silly old fool," he said and scratched his head. "Let's face it; it's a pretty accurate description."

"You're not a fool," Lucy said at once. "Mervyn was conniving, and he was clever."

"Yeah, his wheelchair act had us all fooled and the necklace scam was extraordinary," Joe said. "In fact I still don't see how he managed to lock the study window from the outside."

"I can tell you that too," Kay's tired eyes had a new, hopeful light in them. "I left it open while I dusted. I was too afraid not to. Oh, that's why Mervyn said the theft had to be today – it's the one day I go into the study to clean – and that's why he broke up your jumps last night, Lucy, to make sure you *nosy kids*, as he called you, wouldn't be around."

Lucy and I growled and hissed about that for a bit until Molly said, "Go on, Kay, tell us how he re-locked the window."

"As he climbed in, Mervyn tied a fine, very strong, nylon thread which he'd soaked in lighter fuel, to the window latch. When he got outside again he shut the window, then pulled the thread sharply so the lock slid shut. Then he lit the end of the thread so the fire flashed along it and burned away all trace."

"I told the police I could smell smoke when I went in there," Uncle James cried. "I thought it was a clue, but there was certainly no sign of the window being tampered with so that's when they decided I was either a fool or I'd stolen my own necklace – just like everyone else did."

"*I* most certainly did *not*!" Lucy pulled her arm free and glared at him.

"I know that my dear, and I'll never forget it," Uncle James went to shake her hand but then, for the first time, put his arms around her and hugged her tight.

So, that was it, although obviously there was still a lot of work to do, which went on for quite a while. The great thing about that was it extended our stay, and as far as I was concerned, life was now perfect, with Lucy firmly restored to *best friend* status. Also, a newly confident Evan and Polar spent practically every waking moment with my wonderful Scarlet and me.

"It's been fantastic," Evan said on our last day at Cornell Hall nearly a month later. "And there's no way Polar and I will fail to get picked for the competition squad now."

"You'll let me know right away?" I pushed the blonde hair out of his eyes as we said our goodbyes. "You know, call me?"

"I'll be calling you every single day till you come back here for winter break."

"I can handle that," I said, and closed my eyes and thought dreamily that I'd never forget the summer we'd spent turning Polar into a real hero horse.